A
LIE
FOR A
LIE

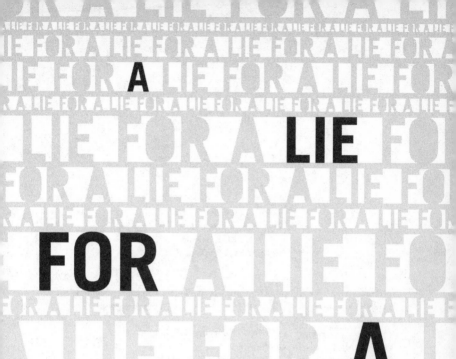

A LIE FOR A LIE

ROBIN MERROW MacCREADY

Christy Ottaviano Books
HENRY HOLT AND COMPANY
NEW YORK

Henry Holt and Company
Publishers since 1866
175 Fifth Avenue
New York, New York 10010
fiercereads.com

Library of Congress Cataloging-in-Publication Data
Names: MacCready, Robin Merrow, author.
Title: A lie for a lie / Robin Merrow MacCready.
Description: First edition. | New York : Henry Holt and Company, 2017. | "Christy
    Ottaviano Books." | Summary: "A gripping mystery about seventeen-year-old
    Kendra, an amateur photographer who discovers her father is leading a double
    life"—Provided by publisher.
Identifiers: LCCN 2016008983 (print) | LCCN 2016035847 (ebook) | ISBN
    9780805091090 (hardback) | ISBN 9781250109682 (Ebook)
Subjects: | CYAC: Secrets—Fiction. | Fathers and daughters—Fiction. | Family
    life—Fiction.
Classification: LCC PZ7.M1118513 Li 2017 (print) | LCC PZ7.M1118513 (ebook) |
    DDC [Fic]—dc23
LC record available at https://lccn.loc.gov/2016008983

Our books may be purchased in bulk for promotional, educational, or business use.
Please contact your local bookseller or the Macmillan Corporate and Premium Sales
Department at (800) 221-7945 ext. 5442 or by e-mail at
MacmillanSpecialMarkets@macmillan.com.

First Edition—2017
Book design by Anna Booth
Printed in the United States of America by LSC Communications US, LLC
(Lakeside Classic), Harrisonburg, Virginia

1 3 5 7 9 10 8 6 4 2

To Peter, Daniel, and Forrest

CHAPTER 1

PEOPLE SAY THAT WHEN YOU HAVE A LIFE-ALTERING experience, your brain takes a picture, and that memory stays with you to retrieve again, and again, and again. Like an old snapshot, it's sometimes out of focus.

When I was seven I almost drowned in a boat accident. If that memory is triggered, I replay it like scenes from an old movie, over and over, upside down, blackness and then light.

Today was going to be another snapshot day.

My friend Jenn and I were at the Old Port Festival. The waterfront in Portland, Maine, had closed down to traffic and opened up to musicians, artists, shopkeepers, and cooks. It was the perfect place to mark the beginning of summer and the end of my junior year.

"Kendra!" Jenn said in a low voice. "That's your dad, isn't it?"

"My dad?" I took a sip of lemonade. "No, can't be. He's in Boston." We moved closer to the stage, where the headline group was coming back for the second half of the show. I shooed a couple of quarreling seagulls out of our way and stood behind a French fry stand.

"Look at the guy next to the amplifier."

A tall man in a Hawaiian shirt was getting beer from a vendor. He was also wearing a baseball cap and sunglasses.

"That's your father," she said, turning her back to him.

"No, it's not. I'll prove it." I pulled out my phone and called him. "Watch."

Behind the beer stand, the man handed a cup to a woman in a matching cap and looked at his phone. Then he put it to his ear.

"Hi, Kennie," he said. "What's up?"

I looked at Jenn. "Where are you, Dad?"

"Hi to you, too. Still in Boston. I'll be home for dinner. I had that conference, remember?"

"Dad?" I gripped my cup hard, and lemonade drizzled over the sides.

"Hang on, honey, I can't hear you." He covered his other ear and took a few steps away from the crowd, leaving the woman holding the two beers.

"What are you doing?" My stomach clenched and my heart began its familiar panicking rise. I swallowed, determined to keep myself from having an anxiety attack. It had been a few weeks since my last one, and I was feeling good. I handed Jenn my drink and felt for my camera around my neck. I lifted it to my eye and pointed the zoom lens at the man in the Hawaiian shirt and cap. My dad.

"I'm about to give a lecture," he said.

I opened my mouth to speak, but all that came out was a weak "Oh." I squinted through the viewfinder and clicked. Still watching, I said it again. "Oh." I must have looked funny, cell phone to my ear, camera to my eye.

The band members took their places, and the guitarist strummed a chord and yelled, "Let's go!"

The crowd cheered. Dad whirled around, looked at his phone in surprise, and backed away. "Look, honey, I've got to go. I'll see you tonight."

"Dad?"

"Gotta go. We'll talk later," he said, and hung up.

"Jenn, did you see that? He heard the guitar. He knows I'm here."

She nodded. "So what. He doesn't know you saw him." She got closer. "And besides, Kendra, he's the one who should be worried."

"Right," I said. I watched as Dad and the woman made a

3

beeline for the street. Now I could see it clearly: his long-legged walk, the way his head bobbed above the crowd, the sandy hair peeking out from the hat. "So, let's follow him."

We stayed behind a safe distance, letting a crowd build between us. At the lights, they crossed the street, got into his Saab, and turned up the side road.

Jenn's car was parked farther down Commercial Street, so we broke into a run, my steps now matching my racing heart.

"What's he doing here?" I asked.

Unable to keep up, Jenn slowed to a jog. "We might as well take our time. We'll never find them now, and besides, I hate running."

I repeated my question. "What's he doing here? I don't get it. He's supposed to be at a conference."

She grabbed my arm, bringing us to a stop. "You're kidding, right?"

"Well," I said, "he told us he was giving a talk in Boston. Why would he lie?"

"Kendra, I hate to break it to you, but your dad may not be perfect."

I went back to walking, slowly this time, and let her keep pace with me. When we reached the car, my breath was as rapid as my heartbeat. The anxiety attacks I'd had since the boat accident were fewer, but when I had them, it was Dad who talked me down. It was our thing.

Jenn unlocked my door. "Hey, you have your freaking-out face on. I thought your panic was under control."

"It was. I mean, I haven't had an anxiety attack since the car thing," I said, remembering how Dad helped me through the fender bender I'd had three weeks ago. He acted as if dealing with cops and insurance companies was as easy as deciding what to have for breakfast.

I shook the memory from my mind and put on my seat belt. Dad couldn't help me with this one, because he had brought it on.

We drove around to find the side road they'd taken, but it only led us to more small streets. Finally, the neighborhood duplexes and mom-and-pop stores gave way to brownstones and specialty shops. From the bottom of Post Road, a street separated by a lush parklike median, we saw Dad's car midway up the street. We drove past and turned down the other side of the grassy median, parking in a tiny alley across from his car. As if on cue, Dad and the woman came out the door of a brownstone and walked down the front steps, and now he had a suit on. I reclined my seat and crawled to the rear window, positioning my camera against the glass.

"Look," Jenn said, "they're hugging."

I watched, hypnotized, and snapped a photo just as Dad gave the woman a kiss.

ALL THE WAY BACK TO KINGSPORT, I WHEEZED through an anxiety attack while Jenn assured me that affairs were common and that my family was in the minority because we hadn't already gone through a marriage crisis.

The speedometer crept to seventy miles per hour.

"Speed," I said as she merged onto 295 south.

"Got it," she said, maneuvering her Volvo in front of an oil truck. "Your dad's been the good guy his whole life. He made a mistake, but he'll fix it."

Sure he would. He was good-looking, rich, smart, sophisticated. And cool. Everyone thought so. A car horn blared and I jumped in my seat.

"My bad," Jenn said, swerving back to her lane.

"Watch it," I said, trying to get my breath.

"Think of it this way: Things that look too good to be true usually are."

"What's that supposed to mean?" I lowered the window, letting my hair whip around my face. "God, Jenn, are you trying to make me feel worse? Just because your parents got divorced doesn't mean mine will."

"I just don't want you to be surprised by the truth."

"I've never noticed anything bad between my parents." But I had noticed her parents fighting. It was hard not to.

"Exactly. Too good to be true."

The image of Dad and the woman hugging and kissing in front of the brownstone flashed in my mind. "I can't believe it."

Click. Today was a snapshot day.

FOR A LIE FOR A LIE FOR A LIE
LIE FOR A LIE FOR A LIE FOR A LIE FOR A
RA LIE FOR A LIE FOR A LIE F
E FOR A LIE FOR A LIE FOR A
FOR A LIE FOR A LIE FOR A LIE FOR A LIE
E FOR A LIE FOR A LIE FOR A LIE FOR A LIE F
A LIE FOR A LIE FOR A LIE FOR
R A LIE FOR A LIE FOR A LIE FOR

CHAPTER 2

I LINGERED AT THE TOP OF THE STAIRS AND listened as Dad greeted Mom in the usual way: a kiss on the cheek, a clink as his keys dropped onto the counter, and the shuffle of mail. Mom answered with her normal chatter about the house, garden, dinner, all the while fixing Dad's rum and Coke. I was both relieved and angry at the comforting routine.

I wanted to ream him out right in front of Mom. I wanted to preserve her honor or whatever, but there she was fixing cheese and crackers and putting little cocktail napkins on a tray for him. And there he was looking relaxed in his suit and twirling the ice cubes in his drink, the way he always does.

If I pretended, I could be happy to see him, too. He could be the same guy if I let him.

I used to see my life as divided into two parts: *before the boat accident* and *after the boat accident*. Before it happened, I was a little girl in motion: climbing trees, playing in tide pools, and building forts with Jenn and Bo Costello, who lived next door. Most of all, I was always laughing. If I had a snapshot of *before*, it would be me running through the waves, head back and mouth open in a happy squeal.

The *after* snapshot is me with my head down and scared of everything, as if nearly drowning swept most of me out to sea and returned only the shell.

I was a kid when it happened. We were on a weekend cruise with Hal and Gail, friends of Mom and Dad's. At first the grown-ups joked about the sprinkles of rain and the darkening sky. I didn't mind, because the claps of thunder were an excuse for me to stay up late and be with the grown-ups. But when Dad and Mom exchanged a look of fear, I panicked and jumped from the bench seat onto Dad's lap. "It's just a squall, Kennie—it'll be over in a minute." I stayed tight under the crook of his arm, and I didn't move while the wind picked up and the rain began to hit us sideways.

When Dad stood up and handed me over to Mom, I clung like a monkey. "Take her, Colette. I've got to get the sails down." Hal and Dad moved forward, and Gail took the wheel. I could hear the whizzing and flapping of the sails and Hal and Dad yelling directions back and forth. Mom and I were partway down below when we heard the boom thudding and rattling and Dad yelling for Hal. Then everything went crazy as both Mom and Gail went to the side of the boat where Hal had been.

I started back up the ladder, and Dad yelled, "Get back down, Kennie!" He was crawling across the bow with a life ring in his hand, yelling over the rail. "Grab this!" He tossed it and went back to the flailing boom. I don't remember the rest, but later Dad explained how the waves filled the rocking boat with water and turned it over.

I remember the turning part. I was below and held tightly to the ladder. I heard Mom's cries for me as the ocean filled the cabin and swept me back into the bunks. Then everything was upside down. I was drowning. I'd been tumbled by beach waves before but had always been thrown back onto the shore and only mildly shaken up. This time it wasn't just a wave—it was a whole ocean—and I couldn't tell which way to go. I held my breath and tried not to let any water get in my mouth. I had to find the surface, find Mom and Dad before I exploded. The pressure in my chest squeezed and squeezed and pressed on me, and then there was a release. I opened my mouth, like an open jar underwater, and I filled up. Suddenly it didn't hurt to hold my breath anymore. It was quiet, and I knew I'd find Mom and Dad behind the light. I floated toward it on a warm current, smiling because it was going to be okay now.

My newfound peace was short-lived, though, because suddenly I was in a rubber boat blinking through sheets of rain and coughing up water as Mom lay bleeding from a leg wound, moaning "No, no, no" over and over, and Gail was curled in a ball crying.

There was no Hal.

Dad held me tight and told me that everything would be okay. And it was all right for years. Even with Mom's multiple surgeries and my paralyzing anxiety attacks, Dad was there for us.

Until now.

So now my life was divided into three parts: *before*, *after*, and *now*. And I couldn't decide how to handle the *now*.

The slap of the screen door brought me back, and I knew Mom and Dad had taken their drinks onto the screened porch. I took a deep breath and released it, letting the memory go with it, and then joined them.

"Hey, Kennie," Dad said. He put out his arms, and I fell into the familiar embrace, but it made me go stiff and I turned away. He pulled me back. "Hey, wait," he said. "Come on, tell me everything." It was his usual end-of-day question. Other days, other years I would have gone on for a half hour telling him every detail of my day, and then I'd ask about his day.

"Today was—" I began, and then stopped. "Hard. Today was hard." It was the truth. I noticed Mom was wearing pants even though it was late June. She'd wear pants whenever she could to avoid showing the scars and having to explain what the long jagged marks were "for the umpteenth time," as she put it.

"Sounds like my day. You first," Dad said. He motioned me to sit next to him. I did, but still wasn't able to speak, so I shrugged and stared at a scratch on a flagstone.

"No, you," I said. This should be interesting.

"You called me, remember?" he said. I looked at the side of his face while he took a sip of his drink. The aroma wafted up. I used to like the smell of rum and Coke, but now the sweetness was too heavy. Everything was too much. I felt like a little girl who just learned that there was no Santa Claus.

"It's too complicated, Dad."

Mom was writing a list of names for the next night's dinner party. "John, we still have to invite the Hubers. It's not Carla's fault Kevin's so arrogant."

He mumbled something and then said, "It's your call, but I can't promise to be on my best behavior."

My mind made itself up. Now wasn't the time to talk to Dad about today. I got up and popped a smoked oyster into my mouth and headed for the door. "I'll grab something to eat with Jenn, and then we're going to the island." Before they could bring up my using the car, I said, "She's picking me up."

"Wait. Your mother and I have been talking."

I stayed put in the doorway. "Dinner party tomorrow, I know. You probably want Jenn and me to help."

"Yes," Mom said. "And we've been thinking. It's been a few weeks since the fender bender."

My stomach flipped as I remembered the way I'd panicked in the middle of Market Square, turning right and then second-guessing myself and then triple-guessing and then braking and getting rear-ended by a tourist.

"We really think you need to get back out there before you make it harder for yourself," she said.

Her eyes were soft with compassion, and I knew she understood how hard it was for me, but she didn't waver.

"Kendra, not driving isn't helping you in the long run," she said.

"I haven't panicked since—" I cut myself off, and then shook my head. "No, that's not true. Today I had a little anxiety."

Mom looked concerned and Dad kept his eyes on his drink.

"Was it the crowd at the festival? It can be too much for me, too," she said.

Dad took a sip without looking up. I tried to imagine what he was thinking. Was he talking himself into acting calm?

"Mom and I discussed it, and we think you need your own car, Kennie."

"What?" *Way to get the focus off the festival, Dad.*

Mom nodded. "We were going to wait until you went off to college, but—"

"I have just the car in mind," Dad said.

My mind exploded with different thoughts. The first one was *Why now?* Then *Did he see me? Should I confront him?* The answer to all my questions was yes. But then I saw Mom. She wants me to be able to move on, to get over things easily.

"Kendra?" Mom was talking to me. "What do you say? Are you ready?"

I nodded. "Thanks," I said. *My own car*, I thought. *Freedom.* I looked at Dad, and said, "Wow. I didn't expect this."

Back upstairs I texted Jenn about the dinner party. From my bedroom window I could see the Hannons' manicured lawn and the Costellos' rambling house and watched Jenn explode out her front door and back her beat-to-shit Volvo out of the driveway past her brother, Bo, who was tinkering with something under his truck. I was still watching him work when I heard Jenn pounding up my stairs.

I whirled around and held up two shirts. "This one," I said, "or this one?"

"The purple. It's more Will's type." She came over to the

window and looked out. "Yup," Jenn said, shaking her head. "He won't give up on it."

"He's coming, isn't he?" I asked.

"Yeah, but he wants to take his truck."

When the Costellos moved next door in the middle of second grade, Jenn and Bo joined my class. Mrs. C. decided it was best to keep her two youngest together in the primary school.

It used to be the three of us doing everything together, but Bo had kept his distance since the time Jenn dated his best friend, Matt. It got complicated with their breakups and make-ups, so Bo just stayed away. Now her love interest was Doug Jacoby. Bo didn't like Doug—and that seemed to make Jenn like him more.

Doug was a summer guy most girls had crushed on at one time, but now I considered him unavailable. He was way older than us—in his early twenties—which used to be part of the attraction, but now it bordered on creepy. He didn't really have a goal, which *was* his goal, he said. After three universities, he couldn't find the right fit. He wanted to go to "the school of life" because it provided more of a challenge. This wouldn't bother me except for his cocky attitude.

Jenn said her skin tingled whenever he was around. He was *it*.

I sighed loudly as we pulled away from the house.

"How'd it go?" she asked.

"I chickened out. It was too awkward."

"Good. It's really their thing." She roughly shifted gears, and I grabbed the dashboard.

"Dad's getting me a car," I said.

"What?"

"And Mom's good with it."

"See, they want you to have a Breakout Summer, too." She slowed down and looked at me. "Or shit, Kendra, maybe he did see us."

Maybe, I thought. *Maybe*.

FOR A LIE FOR A LIE FOR A LIE FOR A LIE
FOR A LIFE FOR A LIFE FOR A LIFE FOR A LIFE FOR A LIFE FOR A LIFE FOR A LIE
FOR A LIE FOR A LIE FOR A LIE FOR A LIE FOR A LIE F
FOR A LIE FOR A LIE FOR A LIE FOR A LIE FOR A
FOR A LIFE FOR A LIFE FOR A LIFE FOR A LIFE FOR A LIFE FOR A LIE F
FOR A LIFE FOR A LIFE FOR A LIE FOR A LIE FOR A LIE FOR A LIFE FOR
A LIE FOR A LIE FOR A LIE FOR A LIE FOR
FOR A LIFE FOR A LIFE FOR A LIFE FOR A LIFE FOR A LIFE FOR A LIFE FOR

CHAPTER 3

THE IDEA OF A BREAKOUT SUMMER WAS A PLAN Jenn and I had thought up to move us beyond our comfort zones. For Jenn, it was going after a guy she was into, and for me it was stepping out of my routine of anxiety whenever I was the least bit afraid. It had recently been triggered by the car incident, and I wanted to get over it. For good.

We were taking action on this plan by heading out to a party on Beach Rose Island, which was at the head of Kingsport Cove. It wasn't actually an island, but it had been called Beach Rose Island for as long as I could remember. It was really a one-acre elbow that jutted into the cove and protected the shore from the ocean waves, but when the tide came in, it was completely surrounded by water on all sides.

Wild beach peas and prickly-stemmed roses clung to the sand and rocks and held the land together and kept Beach Rose Island from washing away. It had long been the local hangout for kids, and it was finally our time to claim it. I'd been waiting for this summer since I'd heard about the parties from Bo and Jenn's sister, Glory.

It was dead low tide when we pulled in next to Will's car in the parking lot. My stomach fluttered as I looked inside and noticed Nicole's jacket on the front seat. I had it bad for him, and he was going out with Nicole, my least favorite person.

"Why does he like her?" I asked, getting out of the car.

"Because you turned him down when he asked you out."

"I should've said yes, but—"

"You did what you always do. You wait until it's too late."

"Ouch," I said, trying to sound hurt. But she was right. I had to admit I did that with just about everything. I could change, though. It wasn't written in stone that I had to weigh all sides and evaluate every possible scenario to make a decision. My teachers called me methodical, my parents called me annoyingly indecisive, and I knew Jenn thought I should stop taking everything so seriously.

So this is the plan. Nothing is going to ruin it, not even Dad's affair.

Jenn scrambled down the path to the causeway. I stayed a few feet behind her, slowing when I smelled the damp seaweed. I loved the beach, the ocean, and all that went with it, but I loved it cautiously. The anxiety I had dealt with since the accident could be activated anytime I was stressed, so I used my usual self-talk technique when I felt it coming on. Dad and I used to make up little rhymes and games to get me to do things when I was anxious, but thinking about him made it worse.

Instead, I kept my focus on Will and the number of times he'd smiled at me, stopped his car to talk to me, and how I was going to let him know I liked him tonight. *Will and Kendra Will and Kendra Will and Kendra*, I said quietly with each step. Before I knew it, I was close enough to see him standing in the crowd on the island, the late-afternoon sun turning his skin a warm golden brown.

When we reached the island, everyone was sitting around an unlit campfire. Jenn and I fought over the only driftwood seat left, but I hip checked her away so that I was sitting, happily, opposite Will. Who was sitting next to Nicole. She rested her head on his shoulder and hugged his arm. I tucked my hands between my knees and looked at the sun melting into the horizon.

"Wow, what a sunset," I said, reaching in my bag for my camera. I held it up to my eye and focused on the deep orange sun above the two faces in front of me. Nicole leaned in closer to Will. "Nice," I said.

Hate's a strong word, but I felt a dark rage when I remembered all the ways she had tortured me in elementary school. She'd excluded me from the playground games when I was too slow, or too shy, or overwhelmed by fear. Her questions about the boat accident and my anxiety weren't asked to be helpful; they were asked to embarrass me in front of others. Like "You probably don't want to be in the band because the loud noise will freak you out, right?" No, I'd told her, I thought band was boring, which was a lie. Once, at fifth-grade snack time, she asked, "Did you see a light when you almost died?" The room went silent, and everyone turned to me. And last year she asked, "Are you finally over the drowning thing?"

Recently, though, Nicole's exclusions had seemed more subtle: a look, a whisper, an eye roll, a dismissive laugh. But they were just as powerful.

I'd thought a lot about why guys like her. She's not really beautiful—she's average at best—but she has confidence. Or maybe it's a power vibe, like electricity. And like electricity, it can zap you.

My coping strategy with Nicole was never to make direct eye contact. My camera lens was my protection, and I turned away from Will and Nicole and focused it on Bo as he set up his grill, his dark curly head moving to the music. I felt better as soon as I looked at him. I stood up to say hi, when I felt a cold bottle against my thigh and jumped. It was Will.

"Here you go." He held it to my lips and I sipped. Beer. It was bitter and fizzy—two things I hate—but I took it from him for three reasons: He had a beautifully sculpted body, he was paying attention to me, and I knew I wouldn't actually drink the beer.

"Thanks," I said, turning the color of the sunset.

He nodded toward the bottle in my hand. "You gonna drink that or hold it?"

"I haven't decided." I took another sip and made a face.

"Hang on," he said, and went over to the cooler and got me an iced tea. He held it out to me, and I studied his arms, all browned, golden hair glistening in the late-day light.

"Thanks," I said, smiling big.

"Sure."

"I like you." I couldn't believe the words popped out like that. I hadn't planned on moving so fast.

He laughed and peeled at his label and then took a gulp of beer. "I'm kind of going out with Nicole now," he said. He knocked me gently on the head. "You should have said yes when I asked you out."

Now it was my turn to take a sip.

"What changed?" he asked.

I shrugged. He'd probably think I was a dork if I told him

this was my Breakout Summer. "I don't know. Things. I just know that this summer is going to be different."

He nodded like he understood, then pulled a pack of cigarettes from his pocket and shook one out for me, like in a movie scene. And like a movie star, I put it between my lips. I held it with shaky fingers while he leaned in close to light it.

"Hey, Will, get your butt over here!" Nicole called.

"In a minute," he said. He leaned in even closer so we were almost nose to nose. "Are your eyes green or blue?"

Everything stopped. I could smell his beer breath mixed with the cigarettes, and even though I didn't like either, right then I wanted them both in the form of his lips. Preferably a kiss. I managed to say, "Um."

"Oh, they're green." And then he was off.

I stubbed out the cigarette, tossed it, and then wished I'd saved it for a souvenir. Shit, Will Beckham made my heart pound, even though he got it wrong. My eyes are blue. Carribean blue.

I walked in the opposite direction until I was at the end of the island, the place where people went to be alone. The sun had gone down, and everyone was back at the pit getting a fire going. I sat on a rock looking at the cottages across the cove, their lights just coming on. Through my zoom lens I could just make out who was having a cocktail party, and who was sitting on their porch steps, and who was having a cookout on their patio. A breeze shifted, and Mrs. Gooch's laugh skipped across the water to Beach Rose Island. This wasn't unusual. She had a big laugh, and the cove had a way of capturing sounds and carrying them out to the island. I followed it with my lens until I located the Kane cottage, and there Mom and Dad stood in a small group with the Gooches, the Kanes, and another couple.

Everything was as it should be.

But within minutes, the breeze that had carried cocktail party laughter now rumbled with an ominous storm. A snapshot flashed in my memory. *Dad, hand on the mast, squinting in the driving rain, yelling for Hal.* The present sky was not unlike that night ten years ago when we sailed off for the weekend cruise.

Blurry fingers in front of my lens brought me back to the present. It was Bo. "I heard the thunder," he said, settling himself beside me. "Don't worry, it's far off."

I held my camera tighter to my eye and squeezed a few shots off. The rapid-fire sound of the shutter was soothing to me, and I focused on that instead of the memory.

"Are you okay?" Bo asked, moving closer.

I gave a nod but didn't look up.

"Just showers," he said.

Thunder rumbled again, but farther away this time.

"So, are you going to do Photo Club again in the fall?" Bo asked.

Words stuck in my tight throat.

He continued. "I'll actually bring a camera this year if you promise to organize it with Mr. A."

Instead of responding, I turned the lens on him and clicked before he could raise his hands to his face. He hated having his picture taken, but this one was decent, I thought. I showed him the shot. He was half smiling, and his right eyebrow was raised up, the way it always was when he was surprised.

"You haven't answered me," he said.

"I'll do it." I got up and we headed back toward the fire.

"If you hand over your camera, I'll shoot you back," he said, hands outstretched. I gave it to him but kept walking. He jumped in front of me and walked backward, snapping away like a fashion photographer.

"Oooh, yeah, work it, baby," he said in an over-the-top British accent. I tried to look annoyed but couldn't and broke into a grin.

"That's it, hon. Let it out, be that girl," he coaxed. I laughed when he stumbled and apologized to the rocks that were in his way.

More people had shown up, and the fire circle was loud and crazy. Doug and Jenn were sitting with their arms around each other, and Will and Nicole were sharing a beer. Dory, from Quebec, was here for the summer. She had a much longer and more French name, but we'd come up with Dory as a nickname and it stuck. She was talking with Nicole's best friend, Lindsay, who worked at Kingsport Café with Bo. Matt was there, but on the other side of the fire from Jenn and Doug.

Looking past the crowd, I could see the moon reflecting on the rising tide, and I headed to the causeway.

Bo followed me over. "You're leaving? Where's Jenn?"

I glanced over to the fire circle. "She's with Doug."

"Doug Jacoby? That can't happen."

"Too late."

"Let me walk out with you."

"Yeah, thanks."

We slipped away from the crowd and onto the rocky causeway.

He talked the whole way, giving a running commentary on that day's events at the café, where he was a combination barista and chef.

Then he asked me about Jenn and Doug.

"You probably know him better than Jenn or me," I said.

"That's the thing. He's an ass, plus he's twenty-three or something, and Jenn's seventeen." He picked up a shell and whipped it into the water.

"It's just a crush. It'll be over pretty quickly," I said.

"Let's hope. Have you ever seen him hang out with

anybody? He's always alone, and if you talk to him, he's all about Doug and what Doug thinks and what Doug wants."

Bo was right, but Jen couldn't see that; she only saw the dark eyes and the brooding artist she wanted to see.

"I'll keep you posted."

We climbed the path to the parking lot.

"Let me give you a ride," he said.

It was sprinkling now. "Sure, thanks." I yanked on the door, but it didn't open.

Bo climbed in and braced himself against the driver's door. "Stand back," he yelled. With a kick, my door flew open.

I hopped in and gave him a look of mock fear. "If I didn't know you, I'd think it was scary that your passengers were now trapped in here with you."

"Just another thing I have to fix on her," he said, giving the dashboard a pat.

We pulled out of the parking lot and drove past the big cottages on Beach Rose Island Road before taking the beach loop back to Kingsport Village. Bo turned the radio on and cruised slowly down Beach Avenue. Too slowly.

"Are we in danger of breaking down before I get home?" I asked.

Suddenly, the truck lurched forward and I grabbed the seat to steady myself. When it jerked ahead again, I gasped.

"I'd better pull over," he said, and swung onto the soft

shoulder. We bumped along until we came to a dirt drive and he turned, swerving around the potholes. "I might be out of gas," he said, looking at the gauge. "Nope, it's worse than that."

"Shit," I said, grabbing the seat and looking at him for reassurance. "So why are you going down here if you're breaking down?"

He gripped the wheel and swerved around the bumps, while the truck bucked.

"Bo, what's going on?" I turned to him when he didn't answer and saw he was pumping the gas pedal and grinning at me.

"Damn you, Bo!" I yelled, and pounced on him, giving him a lame one-two punch. He managed to switch off the key and throw it on the dash. I got in one more jab before he grabbed my wrists and wrestled me back to the passenger side. This was a routine we'd had since we were kids and we knew it by heart, but now Bo was looking at me and he wasn't smiling. He was strong, stronger than I remembered. And he was breathing hard. Somehow this was different.

One of us was supposed to say uncle, the way we did when we were kids, but it didn't seem right to speak at all. This wrestling had a sexual tension.

He let me go and we sat back on our sides of the truck. Bo started the engine and backed down the dirt drive and onto Beach Avenue.

Finally, he spoke. "I totally had you, didn't I?" he said, and gave me a wink.

"Did not," I said, but I let my breath out in a loud gasp and we both cracked up. "Yeah, you did."

"Bo," I said, not knowing where I was going with my words. "Was that weird?" Without waiting for him to answer I said, "Yeah, that was weird."

"Weird?" he said. "Not for me."

He shifted roughly.

"Good," I said, " 'cause that would really mess things up."

He looked at me, and I pretended to adjust my seat belt. I felt his eyes linger on me a second too long. When he turned back to the road, the mood had changed.

Was it possible that Bo, one of my best friends, could have feelings for me?

I said it again, but silently. *Weird*.

CHAPTER 4

THE NEXT MORNING I SNUGGLED DEEPER INTO MY quilt while a light rain pattered my window. Would it storm today or hold off like last night? I played a game with myself. *If it doesn't thunder in the next minute and a half, I'll get up and go to work. If it storms, I'll call in sick, because I'm not moving from this house until it's over.*

I hoped for an excuse to stay in so I wouldn't have to go to Portland today.

Mom went by my bedroom. "I see blue sky fighting with clouds, and the blue sky is winning!" From the bathroom she sang and ran the water. "It's going to be a bright, bright, bright, sunshiny day."

I groaned and went down to the kitchen for coffee. Just as I touched the brew to my lips, I saw Dad standing by the door.

He jiggled a set of keys, and behind him, out in the driveway, was a little white car with a red bow on top.

"It's yours, Kennie," Dad said. He smiled in my favorite way: blue eyes crinkling at the corners, almost laughing. That was his true happy face, and I knew it like I knew anything that was real.

"I love it!" I ran to him and gave him a quick hug, grabbed the keys, and went out the door. White, clean lines—new. Or newish.

"It's a barely used Prius. Excellent on gas."

I opened the driver's door. "How did you get it so fast?"

"It belonged to a client, and now it's yours," he said over the roof.

Pausing, I remembered the last time I drove and how I went directly into panic mode when I got upset instead of doing any of the calming strategies I'd learned. Dad had dropped everything and come to the site of the fender bender. He took care of the details with minimal haggling, even chumming around with the cops and charming the other driver.

"I love you, Dad," I said, hopping in and putting my hands on the wheel. "Let's go!"

"I love you, too, but don't you want to get out of your pajamas first? Maybe a raincoat?"

"Nope. I just need my coffee," I said, patting the passenger seat.

While he was getting the coffee, I sat behind the wheel and ran my hands over the dashboard. It was mine. My own space. I flicked the power locks off and on, and in those seconds I let the image of Dad and his girlfriend in front of the brownstone creep into my mind, but it vanished as he pulled off the bow and threw it in the backseat. He hopped in with two travel mugs, and I backed my new car out of the driveway.

"Listen to this," he said, cranking up the radio. "It has a six-CD changer, GPS, air conditioning. The works."

I drove the beach loop and pulled up to the Seaside, where Jenn was a chambermaid, and called her cell. She came out the front door and ran down the stairs.

"Way cute, Kendra!" she said, still talking on her phone. She came over and leaned in the driver's window. "Will you get me one, too, Mr. Sullivan?" She pressed her hands together and batted her eyelashes.

"Only if you're a good girl," he said. "And there's no chance of that, right?"

"Probably not," she said. She ran her hand along the steering wheel. "I love it."

"*I'll* pick *you* up tonight," I said.

"If Doug doesn't first," she said.

"Let me know. Like you could keep it to yourself."

Driving back to the house with the windows down, music up, we both hung our arms out the windows, drumming on the doors, and catching the occasional raindrop. Maybe Dad made a mistake, but I could talk to him about it later. I dropped him at his car and then went inside to change for work, still thinking about his surprise gift. Without my realizing it, he'd done another pretty cool thing; he'd gotten me to drive through the rain without being anxious.

After the boat accident, he'd worked out of his office in Kingsport. Mom had a long recovery with surgeries on her leg and I had developed severe anxiety, so Grandma Sullivan moved in to help. She took mom to physical therapy and got me to go back to school, but Dad was my rock, and I was attached to him. He was the only one who could talk me down from a nightmare or an anxiety attack, and he had this way of coaxing me to go to school even when I was petrified. When Mom was back on her feet, he went back to work at the Portland office and Grandma went home to Massachusetts, but one thing didn't change, and that was the special connection we had developed.

As I drove the half hour to Portland, I thought about how my job at Sullivan and Sullivan would change this summer from cleaning the Portland office to also being office gofer.

This would be double the money I made last year. Now that I had a car, I would need to keep gas in it.

When I arrived at Sullivan and Sullivan, Uncle Steve was on the phone, and Ellie, the paralegal, was typing. They both gave me a wave as I walked by them to the workroom. I hung up my bag and poured myself a cup of coffee. Still terrible. I'd fix that this summer.

Uncle Steve and Dad were opposites. Dad was kind of a show-off, but in a good way. He loved to do things that were different and edgy. We always went to the newest restaurants and vacationed in different places. He was the one who'd take the risky cases. Uncle Steve was quiet and thoughtful and liked things simple. He had a work schedule that he stuck to, and on weekends he went to his lake house with Aunt Mimi.

I only remember one time they fought, and it was like they had switched bodies. Uncle Steve came over to the house and screamed and yelled at Dad in the driveway while Mom and I watched from the kitchen. Dad made "calm down" hand motions, but it didn't help. We only heard a few choice words like *idiot*, *stupid*, and *liar*.

The memory was interrupted by Uncle Steve, who bounded into the room and gave me a big bear hug.

"How's my girl?" he asked, giving me a kiss on top of my head.

"Good, real good," I said.

"Senior year coming up, right?" he asked.

"Yup," I said, dumping the pot of stale coffee in the sink.

"Ellie's coffee is pretty bad, isn't it? How about you take over that job this summer."

"I was hoping you'd say that."

Besides making a new pot of coffee, I shredded papers, organized the supply closet, watered the plants, and fed Bubba, the resident koi.

While I vacuumed Dad's office, I noticed a planner on his desk and flipped it open. It was the kind that had tasks organized by priority, but when I opened it, I noticed it wasn't his handwriting; it was Ellie's beautiful script. It listed conference calls, lunches, and client appointments. In a pocket on the inside cover were receipts mostly for restaurants, but one from Nick's Sporting Goods caught my eye. The word *Skipper* was scrawled across the top of it. Without thinking it over, I pocketed it.

"Do you need something, Kendra?" Ellie called over the noise of the vacuum.

I startled and flushed, turning off the vacuum and flipping the planner closed.

"Oh, no, I just wondered what Dad was doing today."

"You probably won't find it in there. He mostly uses his phone for everything. That's just for office appointments." She put a stack of papers on his desk and went to the doorway. "He's lunching with a client, but he'll be in later."

I stared at the planner, wanting to check what he had down for yesterday, but I held off my urge. Getting caught being nosy was embarrassing, and I wanted to get out of there. I pushed the vacuum past Ellie and into the workroom, then signed myself out for the day with the excuse of meeting someone.

Traffic entering Kingsport was bumper to bumper because of the bridge. It opened for almost every boat. I didn't mind traffic in Market Square on my first day back. I could take it slow, and from where I was in the line of cars, I watched Will, who was working at the Clam Shack takeout. He was eating some fries and looking adorable while he dipped them in catsup. How can someone be so cute while eating fries? I like fries, too, I thought and quickly jumped to the conclusion that we were meant to be together. I waved, but he didn't recognize the car. When I got home, I called Jenn to tell her about the Will sighting.

"Yes, Kendra, it's definitely a match. The math goes like this: Will plus fries plus Kendra plus fries equals long-term relationship," she said.

"I thought so; don't forget you're helping me with the party tonight."

"I'm on my way now."

<hr />

THE DINNER PARTY WAS TYPICAL SULLIVAN STYLE. Mom invited the Kanes, the Hubers, the Gooches, and Uncle Steve and Aunt Mimi, too.

Jenn and I had strung the sunporch and patio with white lights, and we even put some around the pool. It was beautiful, and Mom and Dad looked like they'd walked off the pages of *Town & Country*.

We served drinks and passed canapés, and soon everyone was loose and happy. Jenn and I hung out in the garden and stuffed ourselves with olives and appetizers. From here I could see that Dad was alone in the stairwell.

"Watch my dad," I said to Jenn. "He's checking his phone again."

"Waiting for a verdict?"

"No, watch him. He's texting."

"It's probably his girlfriend," she said. "He's smiling."

Immediately, I felt defensive. Then disgusted. He slipped the phone into his jacket and then checked his watch. I had to see what he wrote. He definitely looked more like a guy waiting on a girlfriend than a verdict.

"Jenn, do you think my car is more than a gift?"

She didn't look up but said, "It's possible. Think about it, Kendra."

I shook my head, but I knew it was true, and for once we sat in silence. The only sounds were the clinking of glasses and silverware and the summer party chatter.

After dinner the party continued around the pool. I cleared the table, and Jenn scraped leftovers into the sink.

"Dad's jacket is on his chair," I said quietly, "and I know which pocket his phone is in."

Her eyes grew large. "Do it. Do it!"

I handed her the stack of plates and went to his chair, I put my back to the patio door so no one could tell what I was doing and slipped the phone into my pocket.

Poking my head back into the kitchen, I motioned for Jenn to meet me upstairs.

We sat on the floor with the phone between us.

"Go ahead," I said, and I slid it toward her.

She pushed it back. "He's your dad."

"I can't believe I'm doing this," I said as I pushed the menu button. Sure enough, he'd received a text at 7:54.

Skipper: where are you?

John: dinner party

Skipper: don't forget the game tomorrow

John: what time?

Skipper: 9:00 let's meet here first

John: ok love you

Skipper: love you back xo

I slid the phone to Jenn.

She scrunched up her face. "Skipper? He's dating a sea captain?"

"Give it to me," I said, reaching for it.

"Okay," she said. "Not the time to joke." She slid it back to me.

I didn't recognize the number, but I remembered the receipt in my pocket. I took it out and handed it to Jenn. "Check this out," I said.

"Where'd you get this?" She gasped. "You took this?"

"Yeah, it was in his office," I said, scrolling through the other texts. There were more of the same.

Skipper: don't forget me at the dealership

John: on my way

And even more.

John: That guy was obnoxious and his wife doesn't ever stop. Do we have to go?

Skipper: Yes, but I'll owe you.

John: And I won't forget it

Another was too much, though, and I set it down like it was poison. "Oh, gross! This is so bad, Jenn, I can't look at these anymore."

> **John:** Happy birthday, babe! Be home soon with your favorites!
> **Skipper:** Just get here. You're all I need. Love you babe.

Sweat beaded on my forehead and I fought back nausea. I put my arm over my eyes and shut Jenn out while she talked about her mom's affairs. I wanted to forget. Some people did these things, but not my father.

We returned the phone to Dad's jacket and finished cleaning the kitchen at warp speed. I wanted out; I couldn't face Dad. I left a note saying we'd be at the island.

"The island?" she said, looking over my shoulder.

I nodded. "Anywhere but here."

"Are you going to tell your mom what's going on?"

"No. Not yet," I said, and then I remembered his texts to Skipper, whoever that was. "I don't know. Maybe tomorrow. Maybe never. Let's just go."

This time I drove, but all I could think of was the image of Dad texting.

"Kennie, try to forget it. Just think about this car." She ran her hand over the glove compartment and then opened it. "Cool. It's amazingly cool." Touching the energy display, she said, "It's like ordering fast food." She poked the touchpad. "Would you like fries with that? Of course you would, and some for Will, too." The screen flashed from audio to climate to audio, and then cold air blasted from the vents and a CD ejected from its slot.

"What are you doing?" I asked.

She looked at it. "Is this yours?" She pulled out the disc.

I looked it over. "What is it?"

"It says *Mix*." She loaded it back in and turned it up, clicking through the tracks. It was classic rock and some folk. "This sucks. We'll call it Previous Owner Mix," she said.

I kind of liked it. "Go back to the Zeppelin, Jenn. Yeah, nice," I said. It reminded me of the parties we'd had on the beach with the Beckhams and Uncle Steve before the accident. Will and I would toast marshmallows with my cousins and have bonfires, and we got to stay up late. I remembered falling asleep against Dad's chest, wrapped in his sweatshirt, waking only to the sound of his muffled laughter.

As I pulled into the island parking lot beside Will's car, Jenn flipped down the visor and checked her makeup, and I hopped out and gave my car a pat on the roof.

"My car, Jenn. Can you believe it?"

"Believe it. Remember, Kendra, it's your Breakout

Summer, right? The car is just part of it." She turned and ran down the path to the causeway.

She was right; I'd driven tonight without a hitch in my breath or an anxious heart. I'd left all that back at the house with Dad.

FOR A LIE FOR A LIE FOR A LIE
LIFE FOR A LIE FOR A LIE FOR A LIE FOR A LI
R A LIE FOR A LIE FOR A LIE FOR A LIE FO
FOR A LIE FOR A LIE FOR A LIE FOR A
R A LIE FOR A LIE FOR A LIE FOR A LIE
E FOR A LIE FOR A LIE FOR A LIE FOR
A LIE FOR A LIE FOR A LIE FOR A

CHAPTER 5

"WAIT UP!" I CALLED. I FOLLOWED DOWN THE PATH and stopped at the beginning of the causeway. It was half tide, and I didn't know whether it was coming in or going out. Water slapped the rocks, and I tried to remember what the water level was when I walked across with Bo the night before. In or out? High or low?

"Hey, Jenn, wait!" She knew I was nervous around water, and she'd left without me. But this was a chance to practice my cool new attitude.

I started down the path after her, then stopped. I didn't *have* to be in this situation; I had a car and could leave anytime I wanted. I turned and ran back to the parking lot, arriving just as Sam and Will pulled in.

I waved, and they did the nonchalant-guy nod as they

pulled out two coolers. Kind of funny, I thought. I wanted to go out with Will, and I'd heard Sam wanted to go out with me, and here we all were together.

"Are you coming or going?" Will said. He set his cooler down in front of me.

I looked out at the island, then back at him. "I, um, haven't decided. Is the tide coming in?"

He picked up one end of the cooler and said, "Not for hours. Come on, get the other side."

I smiled, picked up the other handle, and tromped out to the island with Will. Sam took a cooler and went ahead of us.

"You're quiet," Will said. "But then you're always quiet."

What could I say to that?

"Where's Jenn?" he asked.

"Oh, Jenn's just being Jenn."

"You mean crazy?"

"I don't even think she knows I'm not with her. Doug's here."

We were close to the island, and I could see Nicole sitting on a log by the fire, watching us as we came up the path to the fire circle. She and Lindsay were laughing, heads together. Nicole spotted us, bounced over and kissed Will, and grabbed the handle from me. "I'll get that," she said.

Alone now, I scanned the group for Jenn and spotted her

laughing with Doug. I didn't bother going over. They were in their own world.

I found a spot at the fire circle and pulled out my camera. I shot the sky as it settled into a yellow-peach color. Usually the smoke kept the bugs away, but tonight was hot and muggy, and every kind of flying insect was out. I zoomed in on Jenn and Doug as they discussed something intensely, faces close, hands gesturing.

Will gave me a soda and sat beside me. The fire crackled, and he waved a mosquito away. When I gripped the can too hard, he laughed. I tried to fix the dent but just made it crinkle worse. What was wrong with me? I hadn't said anything except "thanks." Did I even say "thanks"? What should I say?

Nicole yelled something and Will jumped up. I'd done it again. He was there being nice and I'd done nothing. I was pathetic. I lifted the camera to my eye again and clicked away mindlessly. My anxiety evaporated with each shot. I pointed at Lindsay and Dory. They put their arms around each other and posed.

"Post it!" said Lindsay.

"Definitely," I said.

When I put my camera down, I could see that Will and Nicole were gone, and so were Doug and Jenn. It could only mean one thing: They were on the back side of the island, a signal of an upgrade in Doug and Jenn's relationship.

I'd be leaving without Jenn again.

Bo was here, though, doing something over at the clearing.

"Hey," I said.

"Hey back atcha. Kendra, I need you to document this," Bo said.

"Document what?"

"Le Café Rose de Plage."

Sam came over with a piece of driftwood. "Le Café what?" he asked. He set it down. "You mean Sam's Bar and Grill."

"I like Le Café Rose de Plage," I said. Sam looked confused. "The Beach Rose Café."

"Not a bar and grill?" Sam shook his head in his disgust.

"Cafés have more class," Bo said, heading down to the shoreline. He whipped a mussel shell and hit me squarely on the butt. "Come help us."

A tangle of driftwood had washed up, and I carried the biggest piece I could and set it up as a side table next to a seat that Bo had constructed. Soon we had a rhythm going. Sam and Bo brought up heavy stones and set them around, and I dragged wood, buoys, and lobster trap parts to fill in. It was just like when we were kids and Bo and I would play for hours in his clubhouse, setting up a store with the recyclables and sometimes even real items from our cupboards. I sat in a drift-wood chair and stretched my legs out.

"Bo, I think we need cushions or something," I said, trying to get comfortable.

He nodded. "And more side tables," he said, motioning to the left and right. He jumped up and looked around. "Where's Sam?"

I hadn't noticed that he'd left. We looked at each other and laughed.

"That's so Sam," he said.

"Yeah," I said. It got very quiet. I recrossed my legs. "How was work at the café?"

"Lindsay cried today. Again."

"What happened?"

"She made a caffeinated beverage for a man with a heart condition, and he chewed her out in front of everyone."

"Wow." My laugh came out like a snort, which made us both crack up.

"He turned all red, and then he stopped yelling and clutched his chest."

"What!"

"No, I made that part up, but all afternoon I kept telling her she had phone calls from the hospital, or his wife. It was funny as hell."

"Nobody cried at Sullivan and Sullivan except me. Almost." I immediately wanted to take it back.

Bo looked at me. "What's going on?"

I didn't know why I'd said that. It was the second time in two days that I had blurted something out. "It was crazy busy today, that's all. The office was insane."

Bo nodded sympathetically, but he screwed up his mouth the way he did when he was thinking. I wondered if I should tell him about Dad but decided against it. Maybe it would blow over soon and I wouldn't have to think about it at all.

It was dark, but from where we sat we could see that a bunch of people were around the fire circle. "I'd better go find Jenn." I stood up.

"*Bonne nuit, mon amour.* And thanks for your keen sense of design."

"Whoa, you sound so, so, um . . . what's the word . . ."

"Sophisticated?"

"No, you sound like the Candlestick in *Beauty and the Beast*," I said, remembering our Disney days.

I headed down the back path to see if Jenn was there with Doug. Bo's French was replaying in my head when I heard the crunch of pebbles behind me. I turned.

"Will," I said. I swallowed.

"I wanted to say good-bye," he said.

"Oh." I motioned to the end of the island. "I have to see if Jenn wants a ride."

"I'll come with you."

A path went along the west side of the island. Below were striped slabs of rocks that reached out to the sea. At the north end there was one sand dune hidden by thorny rosa rugosa bushes, where couples wandered when they wanted to be alone.

We heard them before we saw them. Doug's low mumble and Jenn's whispery voice rose from behind the bushes.

"Jenn," I said, breaking into a laugh. "I'm leaving. Can you get a ride from Doug?" I asked. They stopped and Doug mumbled something.

Giggles from them. "Um, yeah, I think so," she said.

We turned back, walking faster than before.

"So awkward," I said.

"Yeah," Will agreed.

He put his arm around me. "Remember when you said you liked me?"

"Last night," I said, thinking about the way it had popped out.

"I like you, too. You're great. Really great." He stopped walking and swung me around to face him. We were between the dunes and the fire circle, and no one else was around. My body knew what he was going to do even before he moved in for a kiss. My knees wanted to give out, and I tingled all over. I tilted my head to meet his lips. The kiss was sweet and soft. Then I pulled away and we looked at each other in the dark. He kissed me again, and this time I ran my hands over his back and arms and through his hair.

I can feel myself going under, I can drown in his kisses, I thought, *but this is where I want to be and it's safe.* We let go of each other, and he squeezed me one more time before we headed back. I pushed Nicole out of my mind and settled into his shoulder as we walked, our strides matching perfectly. I pictured us walking around campus in the fall, fooling around on the hill at lunchtime, and giving each other quick kisses in the hall.

When we got back to the fire, he tugged my ponytail. Then he was gone in the crowd, and I walked back on the causeway alone, not once thinking about the incoming tide.

CHAPTER 6

I WOKE TO THE SMELL OF COFFEE AND WAFFLES AND the sound of lazy summer morning chatter from downstairs. Thoughts of Will and our kiss filled my head until I remembered that Dad was cheating on Mom. I rolled over and tried to think only of Will, but I heard Dad downstairs, saying something about a meeting in Portland.

There was no meeting, but there was a nine o'clock game he was not supposed to forget, according to his text message.

I jumped out of bed and listened from the top of the stairs.

"Can you cut out early and meet me at the club?" Mom asked.

"Possibly. I'll call you when I'm done," Dad said.

I went into the kitchen and helped myself to coffee. Mom

was pouring batter onto the waffle iron, and Dad was at the table.

"Hey," I said, adding some milk to my mug.

Mom stopped what she was doing. "Kendra, you were a little late last night."

"Colette, she's seventeen. Give her some breathing room."

I got a plate and sat down. "Mom's right. I was a little late." I let a beat pass. "But that's because I got sidetracked talking with Will Beckham." I smiled at Mom.

She loved Will. She loved Will's parents. She opened the waffle iron and forked the golden square onto Dad's plate.

"God, Mom, he's so cute," I said. "I can hardly talk when I'm near him. It's pathetic." They both laughed at me, but in a nice way.

Dad pushed his plate toward me, indicating I could have the waffle. I tore it in half and doused it with syrup. Mom was an awesome cook. Her food didn't just taste good. She could create something out of nothing and make it *look* good, too.

"Mom's the best, isn't she?" I said quietly. I looked at Dad and put a big bite of waffle in my mouth.

He tilted his head like I was speaking another language. "Yes, you're right," he said. Then he sipped his coffee. "And she's one hell of a cook, too." He raised his mug, and Mom did a little dance around the kitchen as she collected bowls and utensils from the counter. "You can have the next waffle," he told me. "I've had quite a few, and I'm meeting a potential client." He ran the last bite of waffle through the syrup and popped it into his mouth as he was getting up.

"Client?" I asked, remembering the text messages. It was a flat-out lie. "Hey, why don't I go with you? I want to do some shopping."

"Not today, Kennie. This could be a big case."

"I'd shop and then we could have lunch together."

He stood up and collected his dishes. He seemed to be considering the idea.

"Okay, two o'clock at the marina." He took the stairs two at a time. From the top he called down, "Separate cars." Into the bathroom, door shut, shower on.

Marina? I didn't like going back to the marina, and he knew this.

Mom clanged the pots and pans into the dishwasher.

"I'll finish, Mom."

She gave me a hard look. "Is everything okay?"

I nodded, even though my mind was racing with what I should tell her. "I just wish . . ." I couldn't finish.

Mom kept moving, filling the dishwasher with dishes and adding the soap. With a sigh, she flipped it on and went upstairs.

I left a note telling her I was going to the beach before my lunch date with Dad. Instead, I parked up the road, and when he headed out, I followed, allowing lots of cars between us.

The game at nine was sure to be snapshot-worthy.

———

WE WERE ON THE TURNPIKE, HEADED NORTH. FOR fifteen minutes I kept watch, until he put his blinker on for exit 7. At that point I let him leave my sight. He was cutting it close, so the game was probably at Hadlock Field, just off the exit.

I took exit 7, too, and came down the ramp in time to see him turn left, away from Hadlock Field, away from the office.

Just two days before, I'd seen my father with another woman, drinking beer and wearing a Hawaiian shirt. What if I'd decided to skip the second set of the band, or if Jenn and I had gotten more ice cream and watched the folk trio on the other stage? Would I ever have known?

It didn't matter. It took me focusing through my zoom lens to convince me that my dad was cheating on my mom. Now my focus can help me find out the details, like who she is, and how often he sees her, and why Dad would do this to us.

I drove along Commercial Street until I came to the bottom of Post Road. I could see Dad's black Saab parked in front of the brownstone. After I parked my car on a side street, I got out and hid behind a pickup truck and waited for him to show up. I pictured him inside, down on his knees, begging the woman to let him go, breaking up with her so he could start over with Mom. *It's not that crazy a thought. It's possible that he saw Jenn and me at the festival and he knows he has to end it.*

My phone rang in my pocket. Jenn.

"Hey," I said.

"Don't be mad at me," she said.

"Well, it *was* kind of crappy of you to take off like that. You know I'm scared shitless of water." I could hear her sighing. She was probably sick of me and my anxieties.

"Sorry, Kennie."

"Whatever. Will came just in time. We kissed!"

"Omigod, Kendra! It's happening—Breakout Summer!"

"I know, I know! How'd it go with Doug?"

"Mission accomplished."

"Really?"

Another sigh, but this time it was a satisfied sigh. "Oh yeah."

"Are you guys a thing now?"

"He's taking me to a jazz festival this afternoon."

I laughed. "You hate jazz, Jenn."

"But I love Doug."

"He's old."

"He's twenty-whatever and he's so—"

The door opened across the street. "I'm watching Dad. I'll call you back." I closed the phone and watched him and a girl of nine or ten walk down the steps. She was wearing a soccer uniform with *Longfellow* and the number 15 on the front. She threw a duffel bag into the back of the Saab and hopped in the front beside Dad. So this was his nine o'clock game. The girlfriend had a kid.

I stayed hidden until they were down the street, and then I craned my neck to see which way they turned. The door opened again. This time the woman came out, carrying two telescope chairs. She got into a blue minivan and went in the same direction as Dad.

When they were out of sight, I ran to my car and drove to Longfellow Elementary School. The trick would be to see them without being seen. The school parking lot was filled with minivans and SUVs. After locating Dad's car and the blue minivan, I parked as far away as I could while still staying in the lot.

The other team was from Belfast, and I went to their side of the field. I got settled and, using my zoom, scanned the Longfellow side. Soon I located Dad and his girlfriend walking hand in hand. It was obvious that he was trying to impress her by going to her kid's game. They set up matching blue telescope chairs on the sideline. She leaned toward him, and he rubbed her arm like she was cold or something. Mom and Dad were never cozy in public.

I called Jenn. This was too much to witness alone.

"You'll never guess where I am right now," I said when she picked up.

"You're with Will, I hope." I could hear Doug talking in his intense way to someone else.

"I wish. I'm at a soccer game in Portland, watching Dad and that woman hold hands. She has a kid playing."

Jenn didn't say a word, but I could hear Doug talking about how foreign cars are always superior to American ones.

Putting the camera to my eye, I added, "I have more pictures of them to show you."

There was a long wait while she said something to Doug. Finally, she asked, "Did you follow them there?"

"Yeah. At breakfast he said he had to meet a client, but I knew he was lying, because of the text. Remember? Game at nine?"

"Jesus, Kendra, that's over the top."

I felt my energy drain. "Come on, wouldn't you have done the same thing?"

"No. And you need to leave and forget about it."

"I will. I didn't have anything else to do today."

"Promise?"

I told her I would, and hung up. But instead of leaving, I studied Dad through the zoom. He seemed different than he was at home. Younger. They looked at each other a lot and laughed when they talked. The other thing that was different was the way he sat. He leaned forward, as though he was eager and interested in the game. At home he sat back with his ankle across his knee, a drink in his hand. He had his predictable routines: Kingsport Café on the way to work, cocktails at night, sailing on Sunday. They were routines I could count on.

Number 15's team was winning. She was good. Real good. Her coach yelled her name—Jilly—and she scored two goals. The woman was recording the game with her phone, and Dad cheered so loudly that I was embarrassed for him. The lady next to me swore.

"Damn, that Jilly's good. We've got to come back here and play them again next Sunday."

"Oh?" I said, raising my camera to my eye.

"Do you know someone in the game?" she asked.

"Me?" I said, and laughed. "No, I'm meeting someone," I lied.

"See number eight? That's my Lana. She'll get the ball. Watch her!" The crowd stood. "Go, Lana!" the mom screamed. On the other side, Dad and the other woman jumped up as

Jilly dribbled toward the goal. I watched through my camera as she did a lightning-fast turn away with the ball, as quick and sure as a dancer. I focused in as she barreled past the stopper to make an unassisted goal. *Click.* I got it on film. I looked over at Dad and the woman. They were still cheering. I walked away, ashamed and hurt, my throat tightening with each heartbeat.

Dad was happy.

I HAD THREE HOURS TO KILL BEFORE LUNCH WITH Dad, so I texted Jenn and we agreed to meet in the Old Port at a favorite outside café.

While I waited, I kept thinking about Dad at the game, arms raised and cheering, but I could hardly believe it was him. What was it he'd said? "This could be a big case"? Poor Mom. She'll find out eventually, even if I don't tell her.

I ordered an iced coffee and looked through the snapshots on my camera. Starting from the first shot, the one at the festival, I spun through them, feeling more right and more justified about telling Mom with every shot, especially the photo of my dad and the woman kissing in front of the brownstone. It was the hardest shot to revisit, and I was filled with anger. How dare he! I kept clicking through the photos. Lie after lie after lie.

I wanted to call Mom and tell her everything; I wanted to bust him and watch his world crumble, but what would that accomplish? She would join me in the pain and destruction, and the feeling of betrayal.

And after that there would be two Christmases, two birthdays, two houses, and three broken lives.

I calmed myself by raising the camera to my eye and snapping random shots, focusing on tourists and dogs and bikes, and then Jenn came into view as she made her way toward the café. She and Doug were holding hands and laughing. He pecked her on her nose and she gave his a tweak. They were like a commercial for soda or suntan lotion, and I snapped a few shots of them. I was happy for her, but jealous.

Doug veered off on his own, and Jenn plopped down opposite me, all smiles and glowing.

"Hey, you," I said.

"Hey back," she said, taking a sip of my iced coffee.

"Check these out." I handed her my camera.

She clicked through the photos, smiling and cooing at the ones of her and Doug. Then she sighed loudly when she got to the soccer pictures, and set down the camera.

"I'm meeting Dad at the marina for lunch at two o'clock. I wonder what he's going to say when I ask him how his meeting went. I mean, look at him. That's his supposed meeting. A kid's game with the same woman."

"Skipper," she said. "So I wonder what her kid's name is." She handed me back the camera.

"Jilly. Her name is Jilly, and she's an amazing soccer player."

She grabbed my hand and gave me a hard look. "You need to quit this, Kendra."

I took a sip of coffee, confused by her mature tone. "He's cheating on Mom," I said.

"That's true, but what you're doing is bordering on—" She didn't finish. She just shook her head. "Let it go."

"I told you; I'll stop." I knew I sounded defensive, so I added, "I just wanted to show you the pictures I took."

But I knew I was going to keep watching him until I decided whether to tell Mom. That was plan one, to watch but not say anything. Plan two was watch and, with the mounting evidence, confront Mom and Dad. I needed a plan that was better than either of those, though. It hit me that maybe there was a reason I was taking all those pictures. An idea began forming.

We finished our drinks quickly and went to a consignment shop so Jenn could pick out something to wear for the jazz concert. While she was trying on her fourth or fifth outfit, I got a text from Dad.

Dad: Can't make it—meeting is going late. See you at home. Sorry.

Back home, I shut myself in my room and flopped onto the bed. How could something so good in my life (Will) and something so horrible (Dad's affair) be happening at the same time? And now Jenn thought I had gone too far. The section of wallpaper I had picked at when I had something on my mind had been repaired by Mom during one of her house makeovers, but I peeled a few pieces off anyway. I was working on an air bubble when I heard her racing up and down the hallway. This was the way she worked: aerobic house cleaning. Dad was lying to us, and Mom kept washing his dirty clothes. She rapped softly on the door. "Any laundry?"

I rolled over and pointed to the pile in front of my closet. Watching her toss my stuff into the basket made me want to tell Dad's secret. She'd never wash another of his socks if she knew. Heat boiled up inside me, and I began to silently cry.

"What's wrong?" She sat down on the bed and put her arms around me, kissing the top of my head.

I pushed down the urge to tell her everything and gave her just some of the truth. "I'm sad. Dad canceled our lunch." Tears pooled in my eyes.

She squeezed me tighter. "You know he loves you, and you also know how busy he is," she said. "Think about the good things that are happening," she said.

For a second I didn't know what she was talking about, and then I remembered Will. We'd kissed, he liked me, and I liked him. But we weren't "official," and I felt stupid for caring so much. And that made me cry more.

I told Mom, and she squeezed me tighter. "It'll be okay. He'll ask you out, and if he doesn't, he's crazy." She rubbed my back and rested her cheek on my head, and I wrapped my arms around her.

"I love you, Mom."

"I love you, too, sweetheart."

CHAPTER 7

WILL WORKED THE NEXT THREE NIGHTS, AND JENN was with Doug every free minute. When I wasn't working, I found myself in the same parking spot behind the giant oak tree, waiting for activity at the brownstone. Alone.

I became like the bulldog in the viral video. The dog kept walking into walls but couldn't figure out why. He was holding a box in his jaws that he wouldn't let go of even though it covered his eyes. He tried to run off with it, and *bam!* He'd walk into a wall. But didn't give up. He'd straighten himself out and try a different direction and *bam!* Another wall.

Poor bulldog, he did the same thing over and over, expecting it to be different next time. Just like me lately.

The difference between me and the dog, besides the fact that I'm not a dog, is that I know that I'm kind of obsessed. I'm also aware that what I'm doing doesn't change the reality that Dad is having an affair.

But I can't stop the spying. I *have* to know what's going on.

By Friday I was bursting to talk about it with someone who "got" it. Since Jenn didn't want anything to do with my covert activities, I texted Bo about getting together after work. I knew it might mess with his feelings, but I had to unload, and he'd always been my second-best friend. I told myself it was worth it.

I DID WHAT I HAD TO DO AT WORK, BUT I COULDN'T concentrate. Dad and Uncle Steve had a meeting in the conference room, so while Ellie was at her desk, I sneaked into Dad's office and took a peek at the day planner. Again, there was nothing out of the ordinary. It was all appointments and normal lawyer stuff, except the next week. There was a slash through it.

Before I left work, I checked my texts. One text from Bo.

Bo: Yes, I'm in! When and where?
Me: 4:30 Nick's Sporting Goods

Bo: New hobby?

Me: You have no idea . . . Later.

I had fifteen minutes before I had to meet Bo at Nick's, so I cruised by the brownstone and parked in my usual spot.

My phone vibrated. It was a text from Will.

Will: Still working but I want to see you again.

Me: ☹ When are you off?

Will: tomorrow night.

Me: See you on the island?

Will: K

While I watched the brownstone through my camera lens, I let Will's words run on a loop in my head. *I want to see you again I want to see you again I want to see you again I want to see you again I want to see you again* . . . I wasn't going to bug him about Nicole. It could drive him away if I hovered, so my plan was to see how it went tomorrow night.

Dad's car wasn't there, but the blue van was parked in front. Skipper, the girlfriend, walked in front of the window. I toyed with the idea of going to the door. "Hey, I was on my way home from work and I thought I'd come by and introduce myself to my dad's girlfriend." She'd look shocked. Then I'd say, "My name's Kendra. Didn't he tell you about me and Mom?"

But I was only toying. I stayed hidden and snapped photos when she or Jilly went by the window. My cell rang, but it was Jenn. Not Will. I must have sounded disappointed.

"Gee, sorry I called," she said.

"I was hoping it was Will. We were just texting."

"Wow, someone's getting braver."

"That would be me. We're going to meet on the island tomorrow night."

"Hey, we can—"

"Wait a minute," I said. Jilly had come out the door and sat on the steps, and I snapped a few pictures. She looked behind her several times while texting on a phone.

"You're spying again; I can hear the camera. Oh. My. God. I don't know what to say, Kendra."

"Remember, I'm not the one having the affair."

"Leave it alone. It's their problem."

There was silence on the line while each of us waited for the other to speak. Skipper came out and stood behind Jilly with her hand on her hip. They both talked at each other. I couldn't hear them, but Jilly's action spoke clearly: "Here's your stupid phone!" And she pushed the phone into her mother's hands and stomped through the door. This girl had an attitude.

"Jenn, I gotta go."

"Please tell me you're going to stop."

"I would, but it would be a lie."

ON THE WAY TO NICK'S SPORTING GOODS, I WEIGHED
the lingering disapproval of Jenn against what I knew for sure:
that Mom was being deceived and didn't know it. How can it
be "their problem" if Dad's doing it to us?

I could see that Bo's truck was there already, and I
pulled up beside him. It was just as I hoped—he broke into
a wide grin and cracked a joke about our covert operation.

"Hey, Kendra, I brought the goods."

He passed a smoothie through the window, and I took a sip.

"Aw, thanks, Bo. Peanut butter?"

He nodded. "So I heard Jenn talking to Doug. She's got
a wicked crush on him."

I closed my eyes and sipped some more while he ranted
about his sister and her boyfriend.

"It's more than a crush. It's pretty serious. I don't think
you can turn that boat around," I said.

He shrugged. "Hey, it's her life. He's an ass, but that's not
illegal."

It was good to be on the same page with someone, and
before I knew it, I'd told him about Dad.

"That sucks, Kennie. I'm so sorry."

"Jenn says to leave it alone. I keep thinking I'll tell Mom, but I don't want to hurt her. Then I think I might confront Dad, but I can't do it because I'm chicken." I passed him my camera. "I still can't believe what I saw. Look."

Bo scrolled through the photos, pausing to give me a sympathetic look. "Holy shit. What are you going to do?" he asked. He gave me the camera, and I gave him back his smoothie.

"I don't know." I pulled out the receipt. "Right now I want to figure out what this was for."

"Who's Skipper?"

"That's his girlfriend."

He repeated the name under his breath as he got out of his truck. "Let's get on it!"

There was no line at the register and just a few people roaming the store on a hot and humid June evening. We walked right up to the clerk.

Holding out the receipt, I said, "Could you beep this and remind me what I bought for my sister?"

The kid who was working smiled and waved a scanner over the paper. "You bought her a soccer ball and shin pads, and you saved thirty percent."

I said thanks and made a beeline for the door with Bo close behind. "Whoa, he's buying things for her kid," I said.

He was trying to insinuate himself into her life, like he wanted it to last.

"Sounds serious, Kendra." He slung his arm around me and gave me a squeeze. At the truck, he took something off his dashboard. "You might need this."

It was a starfish on a piece of orange bait-bag cord. "Bo," I said, feeling a lump form in my throat.

"This one was already dead. Promise," he said, handing it to me.

He was referring to the time Jenn, Bo, and I had a crazy plan to make starfish ornaments to sell to the tourists. It was a great idea except Jenn and I had collected dead starfish to dry out, while Bo had harvested a bucket of live ones and laid them out on his porch to dry. It was horrifying. And stinky, too, and we gave him a really hard time. In the end we made about fifty bucks.

⁓⁓

BEFORE I WENT INTO THE HOUSE, I HUNG BO'S ornament over the rearview mirror and gave it a spin. I could've gone into the store myself, but I was glad Bo had come.

Mom was wearing lipstick. She was dressed for a night out in a long silky tunic and pants, looking beautiful. "How was work?" she asked.

"Fine." I shrugged and went directly to the fridge and opened it up.

What I needed wasn't in the fridge. I needed to tell Mom that Dad was having an affair and buying presents for his girlfriend's kid. It was the truth, but way too much truth right now. She came over and put her arm around me, and we stared into the fridge for a while. "Why don't you invite Jenn over and watch a movie or something."

"I'm peopled out. I need alone time."

"Got it." She gathered my hair into a twist. "You see that delicious tortellini salad?"

"Yum," I said, even though I hated cold pasta. Shaking my hair out, I reached for it. Jumpy. I was jumpy. I couldn't relax the knot of guilt in my gut. I knew something big and I wasn't telling. Is the omission of information the same as lying?

This was a big, heavy lie, and no matter how I tried to turn away from it, it hovered around me like a fog.

The fridge motor kicked in, and I startled.

I took the salad out and went to the kitchen computer.

"Is something going on, Kendra?" Mom adjusted her scarf.

Here was the opening. Would I take it? She was looking relaxed and happy, and with just a few words I could change her life. *Dad's having an affair.*

Instead, I kept things as they were. "I'm fine. Go have a good time."

"I'll be at the club with Louise until ten-ish." She left, leaving the scent of her perfume behind.

I WAS ASLEEP ON THE COUCH WHEN MOM CAME IN late that night, but I opened my eyes enough to see her sway a little as she slung her wrap over the post at the bottom of the stairs.

" 'Night, Mom." I pulled the throw around me and sank deeper into the couch.

"Oh, hi, babe." She started up the stairs, but I heard her misjudge the first step. "Go back to sleep."

I sat up. "Are you okay?"

She giggled as she made her way up.

"Mom, have you been drinking?" I went to the bottom and watched as she rounded the corner at the top. I'd never seen her drunk. "Mom?"

Mumbles from the bathroom, water running.

I ran up and knocked on the door. Just tuneless humming. The water ran and drawers opened and closed. I heard her electric toothbrush buzzing and then the toilet flush.

"Everything all right?"

"I'm fine, honey. The girls and I had a night out. No big deal. It won't happen again."

"Mom, this is so weird."

The door opened, and there she was, hair tied back, face freshly washed. Mom, as usual.

FOR A LIE FOR A LIE FOR A LIE
FOR A LIE FOR A LIE FOR A LIE FOR A LIE FOR A LIE
OR A LIE FOR A LIE FOR A LIE FOR
FOR A LIE FOR A LIE FOR A LIE FOR
OR A LIE FOR A LIE FOR A LIE FOR A LIE
A LIE FOR A LIE FOR A LIE FOR
A LIE FOR A LIE FOR A LIE FOR

CHAPTER 8

WHEN JENN CALLED IN THE MORNING, MY HEAD was foggy. After seeing Mom drunk, I couldn't sleep and ended up watching too many late-night talk shows.

"Hey," she said, a little out of breath.

"Hey back. What are you doing?" I asked.

"Running."

"Um, did you say 'running'?"

"Yeah, running. Doug runs. He got me into it, so—"

"Jenn, you hate exercise."

"I love it now," she said, puffing heavily.

"You woke me up to tell me that? Well, I think I can top that." I sat up in bed.

"Good. I need a break anyway." Her breath slowed, and I could hear keys jingling. "It's not about your dad, is it?"

"No, this time it's my mom. Where are you, anyway?"

She let a beat go by. "Guess."

I sat up straighter. "Jenn, did you sleep with him?"

"No, but I slept *with* him, and I'm insanely in love, and I stayed at your house if my mom asks." I heard her car door slam.

"Put your seat belt on and listen to me," I said.

"Okay, okay."

"Don't do anything stupid. We promised each other that if we ever got to this point with a guy, we wouldn't do anything without planning it first."

"I remember." Then she sighed dreamily.

"Okay, Jenn, my turn. My mother came home drunk last night."

Silence. Then she said, "Saint Colette of the Church of Saints? Saint Colette, the saint of all volunteer organizations? Saint Colette, high priestess of the Ladies' Garden Club?"

"Yes, Saint Colette was drunk. God, what would my dad say?"

" 'Let's party, babe'?"

"No, really, Jenn, how weird is that?"

"Pretty freakin' weird."

"Maybe she's having an affair, too." I lay back down and pulled the blanket over my shoulders. As I said it, I knew it wasn't true, but it was good to unload, even if Jenn wasn't really listening.

I could hear her fiddling with the radio, and after a while she said, "I'll call you this afternoon and maybe we can make a plan."

"You want to go to the beach this afternoon? I mean, if you can tear yourself away."

"Maybe. Call you later," she said.

Maybe? That was not a Jenn answer; that was a drowning in Doug-ness answer.

I told her I'd see her tonight at the island, but after I hung up, I had a weird feeling, like things had changed between us. Like I had been dumped by my best friend—for a guy.

But wasn't that how it should be? Would I do the same thing if Will and I were the real thing? In a nanosecond.

I decided that tonight I'd be ready for Will if he was ready to make a move.

Saturday-morning sounds came from the hallway. Dad was hollering for his shorts and boat shoes, and Mom was prompting him by asking him where he last saw them. I silently answered, *They're at your girlfriend's house, probably.*

Then I sat up straight. *If Dad's going sailing, then he won't be at the brownstone.* I called Bo.

"Hey, thanks for going with me last night. Do you want to see the scene of the crime?" I asked.

"Now?" He yawned.

"I woke you up. Sorry."

"No problem. Can we wear disguises?"

"Of course. I'll pick you up in ten," I said, hanging up.

AS BO AND I CAME UP THE RISE, I COULD SEE DAD'S black Saab parked behind the van. My heart sank. He was taking them sailing! Even though Mom and I wouldn't set foot on the *Calliope*, I didn't want anyone else taking my place.

I turned around at the top of the street and parked in the same tiny alley as the first day. I'd brought baseball caps as a joke, but now they seemed like a smart idea. We put them on and crossed to the tree-lined median and hid behind the oaks.

"That brownstone with the girls on the stoop is the one to watch. The blond is Jilly and the other must be a friend."

Jilly and her friend did gymnastics on the stairs and swung their life jackets in the air. I felt for my camera in my bag and put it around my neck and then attached the zoom lens. I leaned into the oak tree, focusing on Jilly and her life jacket. She was unhappy about something. I'd spent afternoons like that, waiting to go down to the boat. It was always Dad and a client, or Dad and a phone call, or some meeting that made us late. I passed the camera to Bo.

"Oh, man, this is cool, Kendra," he said. "Well, it's uncool—what he's doing—but it's like we're old-school spies."

"Yeah, I know what you mean," I said, taking the camera out of his hands and refocusing.

"Operation Snapshot," he whispered.

I gasped. "Operation Snapshot," I repeated. "That's good, Bo."

Now Jilly yelled something and flung herself dramatically over the railing. Her friend sat on the step. I clicked. She looked behind her as Dad came out.

"Shit, that's your dad," Bo said, looking from me to the brownstone and back to me. I pulled him behind the tree.

"I know, Bo. I can't believe it either," I said.

"What the—" Bo whispered. "Shit."

Dad rolled up his sleeves and was jingling his change and shaking his head. Skipper came to the open doorway. She yelled something I couldn't understand, waved him away, and slammed the door. I clicked. Jilly threw down her life jacket and hollered at Dad. I couldn't make it out. *Click.* He bowed his head. Then she yelled again. This time I got it. "I hate you!"

Click.

Bo and I exchanged a look.

Could this be over?

Jilly picked up the life jacket and brushed past him into the brownstone, her friend following behind. *Click.* Dad hopped down the steps and got into his car. *Click.* He drove off, and when he was out of sight, I began to breathe again.

"That was intense," Bo said.

The steps were empty except for two kid-size life jackets.

"I guess the show's over. Let's go," I said.

We sat in silence for a minute.

"Want me to drive?" he asked.

It hit me that he thought I was upset. "Oh, no, I'm good. If it was your dad, would you say something?"

"You're kidding, right?"

"Dumb question. Of course you would, and you have, and you did." He was the one in the Costello family who called everyone on their shit.

"It doesn't mean you should. Do what's right for you."

For a second I couldn't speak. And then I couldn't stop myself from giving him an awkward sideways hug. "Thanks, Bo."

He kissed the top of my head and then patted it a couple of times.

The day ahead seemed empty now. "Jenn said she'd go to the beach. Want to come?"

"Yeah, let's make a day of it."

———

WE MADE A DAY OF IT, BUT JENN AND DOUG NEVER showed. It didn't matter, though. We swam and ate our way through the day.

I dropped Bo at the café by five, sunburned and sandy.

"Thanks," I said. "I think it's over now."

"Keep me posted." He hugged me. "See you tonight?"

I remembered that I'd texted Will that I'd be out at the island. "Yup, I'll be there."

When I pulled into the driveway, I could see the silhouette of Mom and Dad sitting on the screened porch sipping drinks. He'd wasted no time leaving the crying mess in Portland. I stayed in the car, watching and listening to their laughter. Even knowing what I knew about Dad, I still loved him. I loved the way my parents never forgot their routines: drinks after work, dinner parties with friends, Christmas in the mountains, and summers here at the beach. I loved that the pool didn't get drained until Columbus Day, even though nobody used it much in October, and I counted on Memorial Day for the pool to be filled, even though I was still scared to swim. If Mom and Dad split up, it wouldn't be the same. And now, with Dad's possible breakup with the girlfriend, we had a chance of keeping it all together.

I had my camera on and clicked back through my pictures: Dad at the concert, his girlfriend touching his face; Jilly scoring a goal, Dad and his girlfriend cheering. The three of them on the steps, Jilly's angry face. I scrolled down to Delete. The little yellow trash can lid opened and closed, promising to make it go away. But I had to have proof. Instead, I turned the camera off.

"Hey, Kendra!"

I jumped and looked up to see Dad waving. He was blurred by the screen, but I could tell by his voice he was smiling.

"You're home," I said as I entered the porch.

"Why wouldn't I be?" He held out his arms and stepped toward me.

"Oh, no reason," I said.

He looked away.

"Kendra," Mom said, "are you here for dinner? We're having salmon."

"Sure, but I'm going to the island later." I sat down and helped myself to some cheese. I felt them staring. "Will Beckham is going to be there. I think he really likes me." I bit into a cracker and grinned. I was almost giddy, knowing that Dad's affair might be over. I felt free.

I texted Jenn:

Breakout Summer back on track. Dad and girlfriend are done.

Mom got up. "Help me make a salad, Kendra." Dad put on some tunes while Mom and I chopped veggies.

"Out again? Where's my shy girl?" Mom said, passing me a tomato.

I shrugged, but my face must have said it all; Will Beckham made me smile.

"Well, it's nice to see you going out so much. I guess getting you back on the road was a good idea." She chopped into a red onion. "I thought Will was going out with the Marzotti girl."

I didn't take the bait. "He's breaking up with her." I was pretty sure, based on our chemistry. My life was not the same as Mom's. My eyes were open.

We ate our salmon while Dad told us about a court case involving a family dispute over an old forgotten property. He seemed so confident, even after a fight and possible breakup with his girlfriend. It was disturbing.

"So, Dad, did you snag that new client the other day?" I asked.

He wiped his mouth and sat back from the table. "Actually, I'm going take some time off from the office. I haven't had a vacation in a while, and my college reunion is coming up."

"Isn't that great, Kendra?" Mom smiled at him. "How long do we have you for? Two weeks, three?"

"Not sure," he said. He looked at me and smiled. "But I need to spend some time with my family."

FOR A LIE FOR A LIE FOR A LIE
LIE FOR A LIE FOR A LIE FOR A LIE FOR A LIE FOR A LIE
RA LIE FOR A LIE FOR A LIE FOR A LIE FOR A LIE FOR A
FOR A LIE FOR A LIE FOR A LIE FOR A LIE FOR A LIE FOR A
FOR A LIE FOR A LIE FOR A LIE FOR A LIE FOR A LIE
FOR A LIE FOR A LIE FOR A LIE FOR A LIE FOR A LIE FOR
A LIE FOR A LIE FOR A LIE FOR A LIE FOR A LIE FOR

CHAPTER 9

BY NINE O'CLOCK THE ISLAND PARKING LOT WAS filled with cars and trucks. I parked between Nicole's VW Beetle and Will's Honda. I took note of the tide and made my way over the causeway. Up ahead I could just make out Will's shaggy blond hair, flopping as he negotiated the rocks. Tonight I wasn't going to be shy, and I wasn't going to let him slip away again.

"Kendra, wait up!" Jenn called.

"Where's Doug?"

She turned as if to search for him. "He's coming. I got a ride from Bo."

I decided I'd better not tell her that I spent part of the day spying with her brother. "Everything okay with your boyfriend?"

She gave me a look of glee. "Yeah, boyfriend! He's the best! I'm in love." She jumped up and down and hugged me.

"Wow, that's great!" I said, and I meant it. She was truly happy.

She filled me in on all of Doug's likes and dislikes: his preferences in music (jazz), food (he's exploring local), relationships (intense and open), and politics (liberal Democrat), views she didn't share, as far as I knew. I was shocked that my bossy, opinionated best friend had suddenly taken up running and jazz, and I wondered if the change was permanent.

We climbed the makeshift steps and set our things down by the smoky campfire, where Bo, Will and Sam were coaxing it by blowing on it from different directions. Behind me Nicole got up and plugged some speakers into her phone. A Top 40 hit blared loudly.

"I'm being eaten alive; where's my bug dope?" asked Nicole.

"I think it's in your sweatshirt," Will said. As if gasping for air, a flame leaped from beneath the pile of kindling, and then the whole thing caught.

"You're the man, Will. Wooo!" Sam tossed his stick aside and went to his cooler. "Who wants meat?" Most people said they did, but I couldn't eat now. I was still stuck on the fact that Will knew where Nicole's bug dope was, and that meant they were still together.

Sam stuck a raw burger under my nose. "Kendra?"

I leaned away. "Me? No, thanks, Sam." Will and I locked eyes over the campfire, and I didn't look away. I sent a silent signal through the smoke: *I wish you'd dump her, Will.* I half closed my eyes in that sexy way, the way Nicole did. He smiled.

"What's wrong?" Sam asked, sitting down next to me. "Is the smoke getting to you?"

I sighed and rubbed my eyes. "Just a bug."

A few minutes later Sam held a plate out to me. "Veggie burgers are ready. Want one?" I took the burger from Sam. "Thanks," I said, then looked across the fire at Will. Now Nicole was sitting next to him, talking to him about her boss at the restaurant and drinking from a big plastic cup. Will looked away just as I looked at him.

Soon the smell of Bo's burgers mingled with toasted marshmallows and the scent of salt water. It was the kind of island summer night I'd always imagined, and Sam was being so nice. We'd been friends since second grade when we did a rain forest project together. Tonight he was being extra friendly, and I knew he liked me, but who was I kidding? I was only interested in Will. And there I was, stuck on a log, sitting across from him and Nicole. Behind them I could see Jenn pacing near the causeway, waiting for Doug.

"How's your burger?" Sam asked. "Do you want another one?" He was standing before I could answer him.

"It's good, but no thanks."

"Do you want a drink, then?"

Sam was off before I could answer. I could tell that Doug had arrived, and he and Jenn were having a heated discussion. Sam handed a can of soda to me and poked at the fire before sitting down. Flames and sparks rose up and revealed Will and Nicole, heads close together, toasting marshmallows. My insides turned to ice.

"I hate this teeny-bopper music," I said, jumping up. I unplugged her phone and plugged in mine, happy I had downloaded the Previous Owner Mix, and "Black Dog" blasted from the speakers. I decided I needed to do more spontaneous things like that.

"Thank you!" yelled Bo from the grill. "You are a goddess—you know that, don't you?"

From the causeway I heard a faint, "Yes!" from Doug and Jenn.

"Hey, I was listening to that," Nicole said. "Can you believe she changed my music, Will?"

He was next to me, refilling his plastic cup from the keg. "I hate guys who sing like girls unless they're Robert Plant or Steven Tyler," he said, his back turned to the fire.

"Robert who?" Nicole asked.

I smiled into my soda. There was a shift in the breeze, and some sparks floated toward us. One landed on my T-shirt, staying lit long enough to burn a perfect circle over my heart.

At the grill, the guys huddled around Bo. I made my way over, and Will followed. The burgers were gone, but Sam was passing a bag of tortilla chips back and forth.

"Hey, hey, easy now, let's share with Kendra," Sam said. "I mean, she did save us from having to listen to Top Forty." He came over to me.

"I heard that," Nicole said.

I took a few chips and balanced them on my root beer can. The music had changed to quieter songs, but it was still rock and roll.

Sam came and stood beside me again, not too close, even though I knew that's what he wanted. It made me think of how horses stand next to each other just to be close. Wow. Will on one side and Sam on the other. This is enough for me.

But I could only stand the pauses and foot shuffling so long. I pulled out my camera and took random pictures of Bo munching chips, Nicole sulking by the campfire, Doug and Jenn being intense. Back to Bo passing me chips, and then Will.

"Can I take a picture?" Will asked.

"Sure," I said, handing the camera to him. He couldn't see my red face in the dark, but I was sure everyone could tell I liked him by the way my voice turned whispery when I talked to him. Could he tell?

"What do I do?" he asked as he focused the lens. "Oh, this is good. I've got Jenn and Doug locking lips by the path. How do I take a picture?"

I showed him the button. "Right there." He clicked. "Good."

"My turn," Sam said, holding out his hand.

He held the camera up and focused on me. I looked at Will, just an arm's length away.

"How about a smile, Kendra?" Sam said.

I took Will's arm and pulled him into the picture just as the shutter released.

<hr />

AROUND ELEVEN, AS THE FIRE WAS DYING OUT, I caught the scent of salt again, but it had a distinct chill to it. I hadn't kept track of the tide, and I had no idea where Jenn was. Well, I had an idea, but I wasn't going back there again.

I ran to the steps and looked down on the causeway. Water lapped at the rocks. Back at the fire circle, I collected my jacket and my bag and was about to unplug my phone when I felt someone at my side. It was Will.

"You going now?" he asked.

"Yeah, I have to," I said, my hands shaking. Rushing to leave, I put the soda can in my bag. "Crap, my camera!"

"Hey, hey, let me get that." He took the can out and I felt for my camera. Luckily, it was still dry.

"Thanks, " I said, trying to find his eyes in the dark.

"Hang out longer. I've barely seen you tonight."

Because you were with Nicole, I thought.

"Okay," I said, taking one last look at the tide. *I've got fifteen minutes, tops*, I thought. I sat down with him and took out my camera, wiping it off even though it was dry. I focused my lens on the red coals, fully aware of the body heat between us as we sat side by side.

Still looking at the fire, I asked, "Are you and Nicole a thing, still?" *Click.* Another spontaneous moment.

"Kind of. Do you want me to end it?"

"Of course. I mean, yeah, I thought you would after we—" I looked at the side of his face quickly, and then at my lap again. "I thought you liked me."

"I do like you. A lot. But there are complications."

"Complications?" I asked.

"I'm trying to get out of it, but she's pretty intense. It'll happen, though." He touched my fingers. "Don't you need to go find Jenn?" He flashed a smile and gestured to the path around the back of the island. "Back there?"

"What?" I tried to remember if she and I had a set time to meet.

"Don't you have to go on a walk to find her?"

I flushed in the firelight. "Oh. Right."

We got up, and I went to the path at the back of the island and made my way down to the shore. I sat on a flat rock and waited a few minutes. The night was not black but a deep blue, and the full moon lay heavy in midsky. From my spot I could clearly see Jenn and Doug sitting together on the spit of land at the end of the island. My playlist floated down from the party above. I was just starting to think I had misunderstood Will when he appeared at my side.

"Hey!" he said as he sat down.

"You made it," I said.

"I took the secret way." He snuggled up next to me on the rock, and we leaned into the bank together.

"Nice," he said.

"Yeah, nice," I said back, but I almost didn't get it out before he started kissing me. They were long, deep, beer-scented kisses, and they were Will's lips. And I was kissing them. I fingered his hair, amazed that it was softer than the crazy yellow mop it looked like. He nibbled my neck, which tickled, so I gently bit him back and he groaned, a sound that didn't sound like Will at all. Then he hugged me tightly and moved me over so I was sitting on top of him. By the light of the moon, I could see him looking up at me.

"What?" I asked.

"You make me crazy, Kendra."

"I do?"

"If you're going to drive me crazy like this, I'm going to have to talk to Nicole really soon." He pulled me down on him, and I lay with my face buried in his sweatshirt. The scent was light and warm, and I automatically loved it because it was Will's scent. I wanted to lie on top of him all night and breathe him into me. I, Kendra Hope Sullivan, was not scared of what I wanted tonight. I, Kendra Hope Sullivan, wasn't worried about the incoming tide.

We'd been making out a while, taking turns being on top, when I heard screechy, scratchy scales on a violin from the music above us back at the fire. Then what seemed like a kid's song played. Finally, a young girl's voice said, "Do you like it, Daddy?"

There was laughter from the group, and we laughed, too. I looked up into the stars and listened to people comment.

"Play that track again," Bo said.

"Don't you dare," Sam said.

Will started in on my neck again while creeping his hand up my shirt. I squirmed a little. "Here," he said. "Use this." He sat up and pulled the sweatshirt over his head, revealing the trail of soft golden hair along his belly. I moved aside while he smoothed out the sweatshirt for me.

Now properly cushioned, I let him explore under my shirt. I did the same, running my fingers over his chest and down along his belt. He moaned and whispered my name. He was so beautiful to watch.

There was a crunching nearby and we both jerked up. "Who the hell is that?" Will whispered.

It was Doug and Jenn coming toward us. "Hey, you two. Is this what it looks like?"

I grinned big.

"Not quite," said Will.

What did he mean by that?

They sat down next to us while someone at the fire circle played the violin track again. "Do you like it, Daddy?" the girl repeated.

"No, I don't!" Doug yelled.

I adjusted my shirt and ran my hand through my hair.

"Finally, together," Jenn said, nodding approvingly at us.

"We're not actually together," Will said.

I froze.

Will looked at me. "Well, I still have to, ya know . . ." he said, motioning up the path at an invisible Nicole.

"Oh," Jenn said, frowning. "Right. Nicole." She looked behind her on the rocks. "Well, there's your chance." Nicole stood, hands on her hips, glaring down at us.

"Shit," Will said. He got up and raced after her, Nicole outpacing him easily.

Jenn, Doug, and I followed them, single file, back toward

the fire circle. Bo and Sam weren't at the grill or around the fire. My phone was still whining the violin songs, so I changed the track back to Zeppelin.

"Did Bo leave?" I asked. I looked over at the empty grill and wondered where he'd gone.

"Looks that way," Doug said, indicating the bouncing flashlights on the causeway.

I held Will's sweatshirt up to my face to inhale his smell again. He and Nicole were gathering up things from around the fire. It had really happened, but it was going to be complicated.

I turned to Jenn and whispered, "It sounds like he's going to break up with Nicole, right?"

She nodded her head toward the far side of the fire, where there were barely any coals left. Nicole was gesturing wildly and whining loudly enough for us to hear a few choice words.

". . . cheat . . ." she said.

"Go ahead . . . maybe," Will said.

I looked at Jenn. She shrugged.

Doug appeared. "This is way too awkward. Ready?" he asked.

"Do you want to walk out with us?" Jenn asked.

"Not yet, let's stay until . . ." I took a step closer to the argument while still trying to be invisible.

". . . ridiculous!" Will yelled, and he came toward us at the fire circle.

Nicole came after him. "What did you do with my sweatshirt?"

My mind flashed back to her sitting beside Will, looking adorable in her baggy sweatshirt. Oh, god, I thought, holding it out like it was contaminated. *Oh my god*, I mouthed to Jenn.

"Here you go," I said, handing it over.

Nicole looked at me, and then at Will.

"You bitch!" she screamed at me. "You knew he was going out with me." Will shook his head and threw up his hands like he didn't know what to do with her. I stood paralyzed with fear.

"What did you do, put on one of your nervous acts?" She took a step forward and yanked the sweatshirt out of my hands. "You know just how to play it, don't you?"

I waited for Will to say something, but he was already walking down to the causeway. Nicole chased after him.

Then it was just Jenn, Doug, and me.

"That was messed up," Doug said.

I sat on a log and stared into the coals, hoping the answers would formulate for me.

"What just happened? What do I do?" I asked Jenn.

"I don't know," she said, "but we need to kill this fire before we go."

Doug ran down for water, and Jenn and I packed up the rest of the bottles and garbage. That was the rule. Last one off the island does the final cleanup.

Doug doused the fire, and I started down to the causeway. While I walked I went over everything Will said to me.

If you're going to drive me crazy like this, I'm going to have to talk to Nicole really soon. You make me crazy, Kendra.

But it was complicated.

Jenn and Doug joined me halfway across the causeway.

"There he goes," I said, pointing to Will's Honda as it backed out. I knew his headlights; I'd memorized his car. I slung the bag across my chest and let them catch up to me.

"Hey, where did Bo take off to?" I asked.

Jenn and Doug looked at each other.

"What?" I asked. "Did something happen?"

Jenn looked at the ground. "He's fine. He just had to go."

Before I realized it, we were at the parking lot and trudging up the path to the cars. I slipped out of my wet shoes and clapped them together. Looking back at the island, I realized I'd come all that way on an almost high tide without having a panic attack. My thoughts were on Will, not the water.

⸻

BACK HOME MY BODY VIBRATED WITH A NEW energy. Before I went to bed, I downloaded the photos onto my computer and relived the night: Nicole whispering in Will's ear, Bo and Sam messing around, charred paper plates on the coals. But the snapshot of the evening: Sam's picture of Will and me. It showed how happy we could be together, even if I did pull him into the shot.

I printed it and tacked it up on the wall next to my pillow.

FOR A LIE FOR A LIE FOR A LIE
LIE FOR A LIE FOR A LIE FOR A LI
OR A LIE FOR A LIE FOR A LIE FO
E FOR A LIE FOR A LIE FOR A
FOR A LIE FOR A LIE FOR A LIE FOR A LIE
E FOR A LIE FOR A LIE FOR A LIE FOR A LIE FOR

CHAPTER 10

"KENDRA!" MOM CALLED FROM DOWNSTAIRS. IT felt too early to open my eyes, but then I remembered the picture by my pillow. There we were: Will, with his crazy blond surfer hair, and me. I shivered and smiled. This was what people meant by the expression *gone*. Kendra is *gone*.

Mom appeared in the doorway.

"Hey, is that Will and you?" She leaned in to see the picture better. "Beach Rose Island?"

"Yeah, we had a cookout there last night." I kept my eyes on the picture.

"I dated his dad for a while."

"You what?"

"Yeah, a thousand years ago. Will looks just like his dad." Mom waved her hand in front of my shocked expression.

"What happened?" I said, sitting up.

"A lot of things. But that's a talk for another day." On her way out she said, "Uncle Steve won't be in the office today, but he left your check on his desk."

I was half listening. Mom and Mr. Beckham? This was turning into the summer I learned my parents had their own secrets.

As soon as Mom left, I texted Jenn and told her about Mom and Will's dad. When she didn't text back, I looked out my window at the Costello house. There were three cars in the driveway: Doug's, Bo's truck, and Mrs. Costello's car. I grabbed a cup of coffee and walked over.

I heard the chatter before I reached the screen door. It was a noisy, messy home, and it should've freaked me out, being an anxious only child. But I felt completely at ease there.

Mrs. Costello was at the dishwasher. "Kendra, come on in." Jenn rinsed while her mom loaded.

Jenn nodded in Bo's direction. "He's supposed to be doing this, but he and Doug are in a heated discussion about cars."

I gave Mrs. C. a sideways hug and joined in the loading.

"I think Bo's giving Doug a run for his money," Mrs. C. said.

"Yeah, but Doug is right on principle, and you know it," Jenn said.

Bo raised his voice. "That's crazy. Why would you spend

that amount of money on a new car when you can just fix an old one?" Bo argued.

"Two words: air pollution," Doug said. "The emissions on a truck like yours are causing the ozone layer to shrink and—"

Bo cut him off. "Manufacturing new cars, and the shipping from Europe or Asia alone, causes way more pollution than my truck." He threw up his hands like it was obvious.

Doug smiled slightly. "I'm not sure you understand, Bo," he said, leaning in like he was going to make a big point.

I groaned. This was going to be interesting.

"I don't understand? You're kidding me! I know my truck. I've taken her apart and put her back together twice, and she still runs. That Toyota is twenty years old, and she hardly burns any oil."

"It wouldn't burn any if it was a plug-in." Doug sat back, satisfied that he'd made his point.

"What?" Bo looked confused.

Doug clasped his hands together with finality and said, "And giving a car or a boat a gender is sexist."

Bo stood up. "I'm all done here." He rinsed his coffee cup and put it in the dishwasher. And to Jenn he said, "Your boyfriend is a condescending asswipe."

I whispered in his ear. "Don't listen to him; your truck is the bomb."

"Bye, Mom, see you at dinner."

Mrs. C. blew him a kiss while he rushed out the door.

I called after him, "What was that? No hello? No good-bye?"

Jenn closed the dishwasher, and Mrs. C. wiped the counter. I looked at Doug, who just shrugged and said, "He knows I'm right. He's got a serious emotional attachment to his truck."

"Oh, please," I said to him, and ran out just as Bo was backing into the road.

"Hey, wait!" I yelled.

He gave me a nod and drove off.

Jenn met me at the door. "You want to know what's going on?" She sat on the front stoop.

"I'm afraid to ask," I said, sitting down next to her and figuring it out at the same time.

My phone beeped.

"That's probably Bo. He likes you," Jenn said, adding air quotes around the word *likes*. "I beat it out of him last night."

I shook my head. "Nope." I showed her the text.

Will: I have dinner shift tonight. I'll be there after 9.

I stared at the text and weighed my dueling emotions. Sad about Bo and happy Will was texting me.

Me: ☹ What about Nicole?
Will: Working on it.

While I cleaned the office, I daydreamed about Will and me on the island. *You make me crazy, Kendra.* And then Bo's dark expression seeped into my thoughts; like a snapshot I couldn't delete, it kept showing up in my head when I wanted to dream about Will. How did that happen? When did Bo's feelings for me get so deep? When we wrestled in the truck? When we spied on Dad? Before that? It doesn't matter.

Will and I are a thing now.

I put on my earphones and began shredding the papers left for me. After filling a few bags with tiny ribbons of white, I set them aside and cut into a box of staples, paper, pens, Post-its, working fast in time to the Previous Owner Mix. With each song, I relived being on the rock with Will.

When I was done, I picked up my check on Uncle Steve's desk. As I left, I paused at Dad's office. His chair was the same one I used to twirl in when I was little. I made myself comfortable, tilting back with my feet on his desk, remembering my days of writing letters to imaginary clients and assembling long paper-clip chains. One time I used up all the Wite-Out and got scolded by Ellie.

I pulled out the middle drawer to see if he still kept peppermint candies in there. The left-hand section was filled with the colorful red-and-white wrappers, and I popped one into my mouth. Then I fished around in the desk for anything that might tell me about his girlfriend. Ex-girlfriend, hopefully.

In the lower right-hand drawer was a photo album. On the cover, *Early Office* was scribbled on a piece of masking tape. The album held pictures of Dad and Uncle Steve in law school, their first years here in Portland, our two families sailing, having Christmas together with Grandma, family vacations. A knot formed in my gut. It was a telling knot. It said, *Close the album.* But there was no way I could do that, because these were pictures of before the boat accident. *Turn away, Kendra. The sweat forming on your brow is a signal to leave the scene.*

That was what I should have done, but I turned ahead to the sailing pictures. There was one of us at the dock in front of the *Calliope* that made my mouth go dry. Gail and Hal were hugging. I remember them now. He was tall and thin; she only went up to his chest, and he hid her head playfully under his arm. She was wearing a navy-blue hoodie, and she'd turned so that the picture showed only the UMaine bear on her back, and her smiling profile. Hal was smiling, too, and it was probably the last picture taken of him. Dad must have taken the shot, because it's of Mom and me and Gail and Hal. Mom's blond hair is flying in the wind, and I'm wearing my favorite bathing suit. It was a two-piece with boy shorts that had pockets, and I wore a matching bucket hat.

In a rush I remembered the day. The nutty scent of zinc oxide, the taste of salt, the sting of the rain, the power of the waves, and the rush of the ocean as it filled my lungs. The vivid memory nauseated me. Standing quickly, I dropped the album, catching myself at the corner of the desk a second before running out of the office.

The faster I walked, the faster my heart beat. The sweat prickled in my armpits and on my forehead.

These are just anxious feelings. This will not turn into panic. I can do this without Dad. I did it last night at high tide, and I can talk myself through this again.

Think about Will, Kendra. Remember what Will said to you. You make him crazy.

Even though I went over my time with Will in sensory detail and I planned for our next moment together, it didn't matter. The photos kept popping into my mind: me in my bucket hat, Mom's blowing hair, and Hal with his last smile for the camera.

I drove fast, way too fast, toward the brownstone, not home. When I got there, I braked gently enough to watch the woman and Jilly getting into their van. Instead of continuing to the highway, I turned at the end of the road, came down on the other side of the median, and put the car in park. I could see Jilly get out and run up to the hanging plant beside the door, where she dropped something in, and then she hopped down the steps and ran back to the van. Was it a key? If so, I could go in and see where Dad had spent so much time. I wanted to know everything. Like how long had they been together? When did they meet? What was the woman's name?

When they finally pulled away, I turned off the car engine, twisted on the camera's zoom lens, and scanned the front of the brownstone. I focused on the big window beside the door. Something white moved in the lower panes, and I jumped back in my seat. Refocusing, I saw it was a cat rubbing against the window. Playing the role of a photographer, or something like that, I wandered the street shooting the trees, and the front doors on either side of the brownstone door. *Be cool*, I told myself as I casually bounced up the front steps and leaned over with my camera to look in the front window. The cat stretched and rubbed against the glass, and I took a picture. I saw that the inside was nice, but not too nice. I caught an Oriental rug, a dark couch, and plants. The cat blinked its eyes at me and settled on its haunches just as I snapped another picture. I took more shots—the intricate ironwork of the railing, the gargoyle door knocker, the cobblestone sidewalk—and then I heard the crunch of gravel as a car pulled up.

The blue van parked as I scrambled down the steps and started walking past it up the hill. I held the camera tightly against my chest to keep it from bouncing and looked at the ground. Jilly hopped out and passed closely enough so that I could read her T-shirt. *MVP Longfellow Soccer #15.*

A car door slammed. "Can I help you?"

Still walking away, I said, "Wrong house, sorry." But then I turned. I had to get one good look at the face of the woman who had wrecked my life. She was looking across the street at my car, then back at me, then at the car again. Even with her sunglasses and two car lengths between us, I was positive I knew her from somewhere. I looked at her hard, willing myself to remember. And she didn't turn away, either.

It probably wasn't as long a stare-down as I thought, but I was relieved when Jilly ran up to the van, dangling a mouth guard in one hand.

"I found it!" she said, opening her door. "Come on!" she yelled. "We're going to be late for the game!"

The woman got into the van, and I walked in the opposite direction of my car until the van turned the corner.

As soon as it did, I collapsed against a nearby tree to catch my breath. Even though my heart pounded, I wanted to go back to the brownstone. Since they were on their way to a game, they wouldn't be back for at least two hours. My body was telling me to calm down and go home, but all I could think of was seeing where they lived.

I made a deal with myself. If I set the timer on my phone and let myself in using the key Jilly had hidden in the planter, I could stay for ten minutes.

The key was right where she had left it. The door opened onto a foyer with a stairway to the right and a step-down living room on the left. It was bright and warm. The girlfriend was into art, and there was a baby grand piano with photos on it in front of the big window where the cat sat.

I made a beeline to the photos on the piano. When I saw a picture of Dad on the *Calliope*, my heart stopped. Studying each photo, I could see that these people were happy. There were soccer pictures, tennis team photos, and Jilly with a black Lab. Then there was a photo of the three of them on the rocks at a beach with the dog, seagulls above and wind-tossed hair. Posed. Like for a Christmas card.

They've been together awhile, I thought; Jilly looks a little younger.

I checked my phone. Only two minutes had passed. I looked around the room. I wanted to go upstairs, but if they came back, I'd be trapped. I opened the closet in the foyer and found a pair of hiking boots that I was pretty sure I'd seen Dad wear, a winter vest, and a couple of baseball caps. I looked out the window in the living room as I walked through to the kitchen. On the window seat, the white cat twitched its tail and kept its eyes on me as I checked out the bookshelves and knickknacks.

Between the living room and the kitchen was a computer nook and across from it a folding door. I opened it and found a pantry/broom closet with floor-to-ceiling shelves on two walls, and on the third were hooks for a broom, mop, and dusting tool. I shut the door quickly and moved on, bothered, but not sure why.

It was a small kitchen. The island in the middle had a stove with pots hanging above it. The sink and fridge were opposite the stove, and at the end of the room was an eating nook with three chairs. The soccer schedule and a social studies test with *B- Much better, Jilly* written on it were stuck under a Longfellow Elementary School magnet. I ran my finger down the dates until I found the day's game: Kennebunk, an away game. I snapped a picture of the schedule and opened the fridge. The contents weren't like those in our fridge at home; there were lots of kiddie foods, like yogurt with sprinkles, blue juice, and chocolate milk. Mom would never buy fake food for Dad and me. Even when I begged for something in a wrapper, she'd say, "I love you too much to let you eat junk."

My phone beeped and I jumped. Ten minutes had passed,

and I hadn't seen the upstairs. I checked the date of the next game. On my way out I stopped at the front door and pointed my camera at the baby grand. *Click.* Not a photo I wanted to remember, but I needed to have it for days when I pretended this wasn't happening.

CHAPTER 11

JUST AS I PULLED INTO MY DRIVEWAY, I GOT A TEXT.

Jenn: we want to meet you and Will on the island—
sort of a double date.

It was bizarre to see her type out *we* and mean Doug and
her, not her and me. Now I was practically part of a *we* and
I could text back.

Me: Will has to work, but he'll be there later.

Instead of my usual all-natural style, I used the hair dryer
and then the flat iron and gave my hair a shine with some
gloss. *Not bad*, I thought as I added a touch of makeup to my
eyes. *I look good*, I thought, *so why do I have a knot in my*

gut, the one I get before an anxiety attack? Easy answer. Dad, Mom, Bo. As long as I could keep them from creeping into my mind, my summer plans would be on target.

Later, when I pulled into the parking lot, it was half tide, and I didn't even flinch at the sight of the water lapping at the rocks. The scent of salt and seaweed was strong, but it was okay because I had a way to cope, the same as last time—I thought of Will. I practiced things I could say to him as I climbed over tide pools and sidestepped slippery stones, camera around my neck and my bag slung across my body, messenger style.

Before I knew it, I had crossed the entire causeway and was hiking up the stone steps to the fire pit. I scanned the circle, looking for Will, but he wasn't there yet. Sam and Dory were setting up the music and the cooking area.

Jenn and Doug had rebuilt the bar so it was closer to the fire circle, but out of the direction of the northwest wind that kicked up so often. Jenn had picked some wild roses and beach peas and put them in a water bottle, and Doug was burying beers in a cooler of ice.

"Hey," I said, joining Jenn at the bar.

She rushed to me and flung her arms around my neck.

"You're happy to see me, I guess," I said, patting her arm.

The hug was over quickly, and she gazed at Doug as he

shook the ice down in the chest to make room for more beer.

"He's so amazing," she said, as if he actually *was* amazing. When I didn't respond, she looked at me. "What?"

"Nothing. Yeah, he's great," I said, but I couldn't fake the enthusiasm.

She sighed and looked back at him.

"Something's different." As soon as I said it, she smiled and I knew.

"You did it with Doug," I whispered.

"How'd you know?"

"You're kidding, right?" I fished around for my camera.

"I know. I can't stop smiling." She grinned, pink-faced and shy.

This needed to be documented. I snapped a couple of pictures while she posed, and then I got next to her for a shot.

"And what about you and Will?" she said, taking the camera from me and snapping one. "Did he break up with Nicole?"

"He says he's working on it."

As if on cue, there was a shout from the causeway as Will and his entourage made their way across the rocks, his shock of blond hair catching the last rays of light.

I walked through the Café Rose de Plage, where Sam and Dory were hanging out.

"Where's Bo?" I asked.

Sam shrugged.

I saw his truck in the parking lot, but he was nowhere in sight.

"So you and Will, huh?" Sam asked.

I broke into a wide grin and nodded. "Yup."

Right then Bo appeared with an armload of wood for the fire. He didn't look at me.

"Hey, Bo," I said, trying to remember the way we always talked to each other. I didn't know how to act with him now.

He grunted a hello.

"Let's get some wood," I said to him.

He sighed loudly but followed me down to the shore.

"I know you're into Will now," he said, picking up a rock and tossing it.

"Yeah, he and Nicole aren't really exclusive." I didn't know where I was getting this stuff, but I didn't want Bo's disapproval.

He scoffed. "Just be careful," he said, now looking at me.

"What's that supposed to mean?" I knew I sounded defensive, but he'd used the big-brother tone.

"I just—" He picked up another rock and threw it hard. "If it can't be me, well, I want you to be with a good guy." He smiled at me and gave me a gentle shove. "You know his track record with girls."

I nodded but brushed the comment aside. Bo was just being protective. "Are you still my second BFF?" I asked.

He nodded. We did a lethargic BFF fist bump. He went off to gather more wood, and I went back to the fire circle to see Will, relieved to be past the awkwardness with Bo.

"Hey," I said as I came into the group.

Will grabbed me and gave me a kiss in front of everyone. He raised his beer and gave a loud "Whoop!" Then he threw the cardboard from a six-pack into the fire. There was a crackle as the carton burst into flames. Will was a pyro, for sure.

"Nice," Doug said, nodding approvingly.

"I'll be right back," Will said, heading into the bushes by the causeway. "Gotta visit the facilities."

Doug got up and unplugged the music that was playing. "Now, how about some *real* music," he said. He put on some jazz, and Jenn went to his side.

Bo appeared at the circle and we locked eyes. He pretended to gag, and I nodded in agreement.

I hate jazz, I mouthed.

Bo laughed.

I went over to him. "I really don't get this," I said.

"Does anyone, really? They're just afraid to say it," Bo said.

"I agree. Totally," I said.

Bo gestured toward Jenn and Doug. "Look."

They were making out to the music. "You know, Bo, up until a couple of days ago, your sister hated jazz, too. And running. And God knows what else."

"That's what happens." He shook his head.

"What do you mean? Jenn traded her voice, like in *The Little Mermaid*?"

Bo's big sister, Glory, used to babysit for me, and she'd bring Bo and we'd watch *The Little Mermaid* over and over. I always wanted Ariel to get it all.

"More like giving it away," he said. We sat on a log by the grill. "You should want to do little things to make someone happy," he said.

"But you don't want to lose yourself completely. Right? Trade part of yourself for love?" I said.

"Exactly."

"Exactly." I sighed.

"So are we on the same page about Jenn and Doug?" Bo asked.

I dug into the sand with my heel. "Yeah, but she's in love. It's serious, and she isn't interested in any advice from either of us."

"How about you?"

Oh, no, I thought. *Do we have to talk about this again?*

"How's it going with your dad?"

"Oh. My dad." I told him about the face-to-face with the woman, and about the photo album.

"Anytime you need me for Operation Snapshot, I'll be your James Bond."

I gave him a smile. "Thanks, Bo."

"You're welcome. And now for an interpretive jazz dance." He swayed left, right, left, then rhythmically shook his body. I laughed so loudly Doug and Jen stopped kissing and looked over.

Bo bowed. "You're welcome," he said.

Will was waving me over to the fire. "Gotta go," I said, still laughing. "But that was priceless."

"Hey, I'll tell you if you start acting like someone else, you know," he said.

I turned and said, "Hope so, and vice versa."

Nicole was deep in conversation with Dory. When had she arrived? Will and Sam were tossing things into the fire and watching them burn. Nicole froze as I came into the circle.

"Let's not stay. Way too crowded," she said, just loud enough for me to hear. She grabbed Dory's arm and headed toward the causeway.

Will stepped close to me. "Hey, you. Want to go for a walk?" He nuzzled my ear with his nose, and a shiver ran through me.

"Yeah, let's go," I said, glad to get away from the crowd.

My stomach felt fluttery as we made our way down the path to the rocks where we had made out before.

I imagined snapshots in my head as we walked: one with our arms around each other and the sun behind us, one with me kissing his cheek and him smiling, and one where he held my face in his hands and gazed into my eyes. They hadn't yet happened, but they would. I'd make them happen.

As soon as we reached the flat rock, we were a tangle of arms and legs and giggles as we tried to reenact the time we had been there before. It was impossible for me get into it, though, with thoughts of both Bo and Nicole creeping in when I should have been thinking of Will.

So as we made out, I created a snapshot of us in my mind, and like in a news flash, the words *Kendra's Breakout Summer* crawled across the picture.

CHAPTER 12

AT WORK I USED THE PREVIOUS OWNER MIX AS
Will's and my playlist to keep my mind on him and off
Dad. Uncle Steve was at a conference and had left a note
for me, folded and taped to the coffeemaker. Inside was my
paycheck.

> *Kendra,*
>
> *I found your check on the floor in your dad's office, as*
> *well as the photo album. I can imagine how upsetting*
> *it is to remember those days. Don't forget how far*
> *you've come.*
>
> *And don't forget to clean Bubba's tank and feed him.*
> *Love,*
> *Uncle Steve*

I pocketed my check, shocked at myself. I hadn't even re-alized I'd dropped it. *Shit, Kendra!* My big plan to ditch the anxiety attacks this summer was spotty, and this was a re-minder of it.

I got the five-gallon buckets, hose, and cleaning supplies and set up in the hall next to Bubba's fish tank. Usually, I scoop out most of the dirty water and let Bubba hang out at the bottom of his tank while I add clean water. Today, the tank looked slimy so I put Bubba and a little bit of tank water in a bucket so I could clean the algae off the glass.

Soon I had a rhythm going for draining the tank: fill a bucket, clamp the hose, empty it in the sink, repeat. But every time I walked by Uncle Steve's office I had an urge to go in and look at the album on his desk. It was anxiety provok-ing, and I tried to focus on the job at hand, but the photo of us before the trip kept popping into my mind.

Bubba looked unhappy in his tiny bit of water, so I set the hose in his bucket and unclamped it. Dirty or not, the extra water made him perk up. While the bucket filled, I ran to Uncle Steve's office to get the album.

I flipped through quickly until I got to the photo. Imme-diately, a memory washed over me and I was drowning again. In my mind I heard the boom rattling, saw the lightning flash, and heard the panicky yelling from the deck above. What were they saying?

It didn't matter now; I was here to clean.

A sloshing sound brought me back to the office.

It was the tank water! The bucket was overflowing and Bubba was flopping on the floor. I ran to him. His panicked eyes bulged and his gills opened and closed as he struggled for water. I dropped him into the bucket and clamped the hose.

I'd almost killed him. *I'm so sorry, Bubba. You didn't deserve that.*

I decided right then that when I was done cleaning up. I would get some answers about this affair Dad was having.

THE IDEA WAS TO JUST LOOK IN THE WINDOWS again, to see more of the house where Dad had another life, but peeking into the living room would never be enough now that I'd been inside.

I watched the door and the picture window for a few minutes. Based on the soccer schedule, they should be gone for the afternoon practice, but I wanted to feel sure. When I didn't see any activity for a few minutes, I went across the street, looking up and down the block to make sure no cars were coming. I took the key from where it was hidden in the planter and let myself in. The air-conditioned brownstone was a cool relief from the heat of Portland. I took a step down into the living room, but as soon as I did, I knew it was a mistake.

I heard running feet coming from the kitchen, so I leaped back to the foyer and ducked into the coat closet.

"Mom!" Jilly yelled.

Footsteps brushed by as I worked myself silently between the coats until I was against the closet's back wall.

"Mom?" she said more quietly.

Then I heard muffled voices. Someone was with her. Running feet came by again, and the girls talked back and forth, but I couldn't understand.

Steps came close to the closet, and I stuffed myself behind some winter jackets. "I have to get my skateboard first," Jilly said. The door opened and she grabbed it. I stayed frozen between the down jackets until she closed the door. I heard the skateboard clatter on the ground, and then the sound of her riding it across the floor. When she pounded up the stairs, I was still frozen and unable to breath.

When I heard two pairs of feet pounding above me, I worked my way out of the coats and opened the door, whacking a skateboard helmet and sending it rattling across the floor.

"That must be Mom. We've gotta go!" Jilly said, running down the stairs.

"Coach B. will kill us if we're late again," her friend said.

The feet stopped and I stayed frozen.

"Mom?" Jilly called. "Oh, here she comes," she said, and there was the sound of the girls gathering skateboards and hoisting duffel bags. When the front door slammed and the excited chatter of the girls left, I finally took a deep breath. I gave myself to the count of thirty before I peeked out the closet door.

I stood in the middle of the foyer and looked up the stairs. With Dad at a conference with Uncle Steve, and Jilly and her mom at soccer, there wasn't a chance of getting caught.

With shaky legs I crept up the stairs, snapping photos of Asian artifacts and primitive paintings by Jilly. At the head of the stairs was a bathroom and, beside it, Jilly's bedroom. Her bunk bed was unmade, and she'd left laundry in random piles. Clothes and junk everywhere. A quick movement from the corner made me cry out. It was a rat in a cage. A white rat with red eyes. It raised itself up on its haunches and sniffed the air and then darted into a tunnel. I took a picture of the rat. The sign on the cage said *Rex*.

I backed out of the room and went down the hall to the master bedroom. Two large windows faced the street, and opposite them a king-size bed dominated the room.

So, this is where it happened, where my father wasn't my father. Beside the dresser, on a chair, lay Dad's sweater and jeans. A pair of shoes sat at the foot of the bed.

A framed picture on the bedside table drew me like a

magnet. I had to see it for myself. My face went hot. It was of the woman and Dad, silhouetted against a late-day sun.

It had been a fight, not a breakup.

Smacking it facedown, I heard the tinkling of broken glass. I gasped, lifting the frame gingerly. Yes, I'd broken it.

My phone beeped a text.

Jenn: Can I borrow your black T-shirt?
Me: Yes, come over in 45.

Back home I thought about the close call I'd had and my new shots of Jilly's art and the ones of the bedroom. One minute I was intrigued, and the next I wanted to delete them and pretend the affair wasn't happening, but it was.

My camera, the thing I loved so much, felt like a bomb, or at least infected with a deadly bacteria. I wanted all the photos gone, from the day of the festival to today's investigation of the brownstone, but I deleted only one. The one Jenn took of me as I watched Dad, the woman, and Jilly at the brownstone. My mouth was slightly open, as if I was trying to speak but couldn't, my eyebrows scrunched in confusion. *Open. Select. Delete.*

I plugged my camera in to my computer, made a folder called Operation Snapshot, and dragged the photos in. My camera was clean again, but now my computer was contaminated.

Instead of dealing with it, I texted Will.

Me: I'm thinking about the island and us. When will
I see you again?
Will: Yup.

What did he mean? Was he thinking about me, too? Or did he mean, yup, he was going out to the island tonight?

Me: Great! See you there!

Jenn burst through my door just as I pressed Send. While she changed out of her sweatshirt and into my black T-shirt, she gave me a play-by-play of Doug's yearlong plan to study the effects of music on the growth of plants.

I was listening, but I was also looking at photos of the island. Specifically, comparing shots of Will with Nicole and the shot of Will with me.

"Will looks happy when he's with me, don't you think?" I asked.

Jenn bent over my shoulder. "Definitely, but you need more than one photo. I'll take care of that," she said.

LIE FOR A LIE FOR A LIE FOR A LIE FOR A
FOR A LIE FOR A LIE FOR A LIE FOR A LIE
LIE FOR A LIE FOR A LIE FOR A LIE FOR A LIE
RA LIE FOR A LIE FOR A LIE FOR A
FOR A LIE FOR A LIE FOR A LIE FOR A
RA LIE FOR A LIE FOR A LIE FOR A LIE
FOR A LIE FOR A LIE FOR A LIE FOR A LIE FOR

CHAPTER 13

WHEN DAD SAID HE WANTED TO TAKE TIME OFF TO be with his family, I didn't think he actually meant it. Now he was hanging around the house a lot, and he and Mom were doing extra things together, like inviting people over at cocktail hour and going to the club for lunch.

At breakfast he made noises about spending the day together.

"I've got to work, Dad," I said, pretending to read the paper.

"You can make up your hours anytime. How about we go to the White Mountains? We can rent horses and do some trail riding."

Now I was pissed. Horses were an issue. I had done riding therapy for a few years, and it was the one thing Dad wouldn't do with me. He hated horses. Mom and I did it together exclusively.

I stood up and looked him in the eyes. He held my gaze without flinching.

What I wanted to say was, "It's not going to work, Dad."

What I said was, "I have to work on something." Vague, lame, clearly an excuse to not be around them.

I went out the door, leaving my untouched eggs and bacon for Mom.

I drove like a crazy person. Like Jenn. In and out of traffic, my radio blasting, past slowpoke out-of-staters, horn beeping if they didn't get out of my way soon enough. This was heart-pounding, and part of me liked it. The feeling was different from the anxiety that made me shake and get out of breath.

I was in control of this crazy.

I took the exit to the office, hitting the ramp too fast and squealing my tires.

Just because you're doing the family thing with Mom and me this week, doesn't mean I've forgotten about the affair you're having the rest of the time, Dad.

Ellie was relieved to see me and set me up in the work-room with a pile of shredding to do. This was what I needed, mindless cutting and shredding.

I filled a couple of bags before lunch, checking my phone constantly for texts or missed calls from Will in the hope that we would be meeting later. There was nothing. From anybody.

It was also one of the days that Jilly's soccer team would play again.

That knowledge, along with the memory of Dad's favorite sweater slung so casually over the bedroom chair in the brownstone, and his phony sweetness to Mom lately, made me want to do more spying.

THIS TIME I PARKED AROUND THE CORNER, AND when I saw that the blue van wasn't there, I walked down the sidewalk, retrieved the key, and slipped into the foyer, as if it were my apartment.

I knew they were at an away soccer game.

It was cool, like before, and I stepped down into the living room and went to the photos. I turned the ones with Dad in them toward the wall and put my camera to my eye. It was a shot that said something.

Click.

Upstairs I greeted the red-eyed rat with a glare and took a close up of his face.

Click.

He scurried into his tunnel and then poked his head back out.

Click.

By the looks of Jilly's schoolbooks and homework, she was in fourth or fifth grade. All of the sports paraphernalia and science experiments were evidence that she was half jock and half nature girl. Poking out from under her mess of bedding was a teddy bear with a red tartan vest. I felt an urge to pick it up and tuck it into bed, but then I noticed some junk sticking out from under the bed. A violin case, dusty and half-closed, a lesson book, a corn chip bag, a crusted-over bowl of something—possibly ice cream—and a pink diary with a key.

Excited, I opened the diary.

Dear Diary,
I don't know why Mom gave this to me cuz everyone knows I hate pink!!!
Your owner,
Jilly

I threw it back and left her room. In the bathroom, I opened the mirrored medicine cabinet carefully so I wouldn't leave fingerprints, and looked over the contents: women's face creams, ibuprofen, teeth whitener, and aftershave. I stood back and took a picture of myself taking a picture of the sink, counter, and medicine cabinet. I was a journalist on the job; this had to be documented to be believed.

Back downstairs I took in every corner of the brownstone, snapping as I went. In the living room I spotted Dad's boat shoes under the coffee table in front of the fireplace. They'd been kicked off casually, and one rested on top of the other. I slipped my feet into them the way I used to when I was little. It still had the same effect on me: I felt safe from monsters and protected from the world. But now it was Dad who was being a monster.

I thought back to the day Mom, Dad, and I got matching white-soled shoes for a boat trip. On the way home from L.L. Bean's, we excitedly planned for a weekend cruise with Hal and Gail.

Dad had said, "If this goes well, we can do other trips, and then . . ." He'd paused and looked at Mom. "Should I tell her?"

"What, what, what, Daddy? Tell me what?" I bounced up and down in the backseat.

"How would you like to go to a place that's warm and has palm trees and coconuts and water that's bluer than your eyes, that doesn't have school, and where you can swim every day?" In the rearview mirror, I could see his eyes crinkle as he smiled at me. He nodded his head, encouraging me to answer. "What do you say, champ? There'd be no cars, no people, no noise."

I wasn't sure what it meant, but if I didn't have to go to school, I would be relieved. Mom turned to me in the back-seat. "Daddy wants to sail the *Calliope* to the Caribbean. It would be our home all year."

What would happen to the house and my friends? I looked out the car window and watched the traffic for a while.

"We'll only go if my two favorite girls want to go." He raised his eyebrows. "What do you say, Kennie? You already have Caribbean-blue eyes, you know."

I took my new shoes out of the box and put them on with-out socks, just the way Dad wore them. Then I heard him say, "Let's do it."

Mom turned to him and smiled. "Yeah, let's."

My alarm snapped me back to the now, and I replaced Dad's shoes and left the brownstone. The elation I felt from spying was gone, and I was left with a dark emptiness.

On my way to the car I thought about Grandma Sullivan, Dad's mom. When she helped us after the accident, she was better than a grandma. She was like an aunt and a sister all in one, and I could always talk to her, so I decided to call. I needed someone wise to tell me what to do.

"Kennie, my girl, how are you?" she said. Her voice was

soft and lilting in the way I remembered. I'd pulled over to Harbor Park to make the call. Bikes, Rollerblades, and skateboards filled the paths around the grassy park.

"Not good, Grandma."

"Oh dear. What can I do? Tell me," she said, sighing into the phone.

"It's about Dad." I began to cry. "I'm sorry, Grandma, I don't know what to do."

There was a deep sigh and then she said, "Go ahead, honey."

"I saw Dad with another woman. It's not a mistake. He's definitely involved with her. I don't know what to do. I haven't said anything to Mom or Dad." At that moment I wanted to be on her lap, five years old again, being rocked while I cried, not three states away.

She didn't say anything.

"Grandma? Are you there?"

Silence on the other end, and then, "What can I do?"

"I don't know what to do. I was hoping it was a mistake, but it's not."

"This isn't something you should have to deal with." She harrumphed into the phone. "Let me try to help."

I sniffed. "What are you going to do?"

"I'll call him and give him a talking-to—that's what I'll do." She laughed. "Don't worry, Kennie."

"No, please don't. He can't know I know, Grandma. I just want to know what to do. Please don't tell him I know!"

"Kendra, you did nothing wrong; let's get that straight right away. He needs to deal with this, not you."

"Grandma," I said, gathering my strength, "let me handle this on my own. I shouldn't have told you."

She sighed into the phone. "Nonsense."

"I'll take care of it. Just promise me you'll wait, Grandma."

"Well," she said, "if I don't hear from you in a few days, I'm going to call him."

"Deal," I said. I hung up, knowing just the person who could help me.

WHEN I GOT HOME, I TEXTED BO.

> **Me:** Kendra calling James Bond.
> **Bo:** Bond here. Is this about Operation Snapshot?
> **Me:** I want to heat things up, but I need your expertise.
> **Bo:** Come to the cafe tomorrow morning.

FOR A LIE FOR A LIE FOR A LIE
FOR A LIE FOR A LIE FOR A LIE FOR A LIE
R A LIE FOR A LIE FOR A LIE FO
FOR A LIE FOR A LIE FOR A
R A LIE FOR A LIE FOR A LIE FOR A LIE
FOR A LIE FOR A LIE FOR A LIE FOR

CHAPTER 14

ON THE WAY TO THE CAFÉ, I WORKED OUT WHAT I
wanted to do: freak Dad out by sending photos of him and
Skipper to his phone. I just didn't know how to do it without
getting caught, but I was sure when he found out someone
knew about the affair, he would have to stop.

Bo would know how to set this up so that I wouldn't be
found out.

This plan gave me the kind of adrenaline rush that
would've led to an anxiety attack last year but now just felt
like a tingle of electricity instead of a heart-stopping zap.

There was a line at the café. I stood in line behind an old
couple who were taking a long time to decide what size
coffees to order.

"You want a large? It's called a grande," Bo said.

"I want the biggest," the man said.

"Okay, that's the sixteen-ounce," Bo said.

"Is sixteen ounces the same as the grand one?"

"Yes. And you, ma'am?"

"I'd like a small with milk, please," she said.

Bo turned to Lindsay. "And a tall, too."

"No, I said *small* coffee, with milk, please," the woman said loudly.

Bo looked at me and tried to keep from smiling. "A tall is a small."

The old couple looked at each other.

"I know, it's stupid. Just trust me," Bo said.

He filled their orders and signaled "five minutes" to Lindsay.

When he sat down, I lowered my voice and said, "I need to talk to you about something big. About a plan to mess with my dad."

He gave me an exaggerated wink. "Are we going to spy again?"

"No, I have another idea, but I'm not sure how to do it without getting caught," I said.

"Will I like it?" Bo asked.

"I think so. Remember the day you went with me to the brownstone in Portland?"

He nodded.

"Well, I took some more pictures."

He raised his eyebrows.

"Inside," I added.

"Badass."

"Jenn doesn't know."

Bo nodded and leaned forward. "What do you want to do?"

I told him my idea about sending Dad pictures.

Bo leaned forward. "I know exactly what to do. I saw it in a movie. You just buy a burner phone." He held out his arms, satisfied, like he was waiting for applause.

"Okay, but then what?"

"You send whatever pictures you want to the new phone and then send them to your dad's number."

"He can't trace it to me?"

Bo shook his head.

My stomach flipped. It was so easy. "Let's do it."

"I'll be over after work."

———

IT WAS TURNING OUT TO BE A GREAT DAY. BESIDES Bo solving my technology problem, Mom and Dad were in the White Mountains for the afternoon, and maybe that would bring them together again.

And now Will was texting me that he was going to be on the island tonight. His exact text was: *NO NICOLE.*

Later, Bo arrived with a new phone, and we set it up. I tranferred the picture of Dad and the girlfriend at the festival to the new phone. All I had to do was send it.

"Thanks, Bo!" I hugged him.

He didn't hug back.

"Oh, sorry," I said.

"It's okay. I like your hugs."

I stammered a few syllables of an apology. My finger paused over the Send button on the burner phone.

"But you're still with Will, right?" he asked.

I nodded. "I'm going to see him at the island tonight."

"Okay. So this is just friends?" He gestured between the two of us sitting at the computer.

I felt a sinking in my gut. "Just friends."

As soon as I said it, he got up and walked to the door. "Can I say something?" Bo asked. "As a friend?"

I nodded but silently wished I didn't have to hear it. I looked at the new phone, turning it over.

"Careful," he said.

He was standing in the doorway.

"Yeah, this could go south quickly," I said, indicating the phone, but I knew he wasn't talking about that.

He shook his head, his brown curls brushing against the door frame.

"I know you're all about Will, but he's—"

"What? He said he was crazy about me. We're together."

"Hey, calm down. I know how you feel." He turned to go and then said, "Remember, just don't forget yourself."

I rolled my eyes at the drama, but then a snapshot from *The Little Mermaid* came to mind.

He's reminding me not to lose my voice.

I hit Send.

The response from Dad didn't come right away. I didn't know what I'd expected. I set the phone aside and plopped on my bed. Bo's words were just a whisper compared to Will's text in all caps.

I didn't want to wait until the usual after-dark party.

Me: I'm heading to Beach Rose right now.

Will: I'll be there in fifteen babe.

He called me babe. Babe!

———————

I PULLED IN BESIDE WILL'S HONDA. HE MOTIONED for me to get in the passenger side. I had barely sat down when he flung himself over me. Reaching around, he moved a lever and dropped my seat down with a jolt.

I was looking up into the lightest blue eyes I'd ever seen.

They were almost gray, and I hadn't realized. We'd only been close in the dark, and in secret. Now there was no Nicole, and we didn't have to hide.

He kissed my neck and then moved quickly down my chest, between my breasts. Before I could stop him, he'd flipped my T-shirt up and over my head, pulling my hair forward and leaving it around my shoulders.

"Damn, you're hot, Kendra," he said, staring down at me.

My hands went immediately over my breasts.

"Don't," he said, holding my wrists. He held them above my head and kissed me deeply.

I was kissing him back but wasn't really into it because I was worrying about someone pulling up beside us.

That's exactly what happened. A truck pulled up on his side of the Honda.

"Shit, Will, stop," I said, pushing him away and pulling my shirt back on.

He groaned and slid into the driver's seat. I brought my seat upright and looked across at Sam and Dory.

Without missing a beat, Will had his window down and he and Sam were making plans for the evening. The mackerel were running, and they wanted to catch them off the bridge.

Sam backed out and Will started his engine. I looked at

him, waiting to see whether I was included. When the car moved, I motioned for him to stop.

"Hey, I've gotta be somewhere. I'll text you later," I said.

"That's cool, babe," he said.

I leaned in and kissed him.

He left, and I leaned against my car and stared at the island. He'd acted as if that make-out session was what people did. If so, why didn't it feel right?

I shook it off. He obviously liked me.

Will and Kendra had to be for real.

CHAPTER 15

BEFORE WORK THE NEXT DAY, I STOPPED AT THE café. Lindsay and Bo were busy behind the counter, but I wanted to make sure things were cool between us, especially since Will and I were now out in the open.

Bo seemed tired and a little melancholy today, not his funny self. There is no law that says we have to play our childhood role for our whole lives; otherwise I would be a panicky mess and he would be an annoying class clown.

He spotted me and gave me a quick smile. His eyes lit up, so I knew things were good. I went to a table and he came over.

"Hey," he said, "you don't have to tell me. I already know."

I must have looked confused. He sat and stretched his long legs into the aisle.

"Sam told me," he said, giving the table a swipe with his dishrag.

"Oh, right." I fumbled for what to say. Finally, I settled on an apology. Our confusing friendship was my fault. "I'm sorry about the other night," I said. "I know you were just trying to help." Bo was looking deeply into my eyes. "About forgetting myself." The way he was staring was so disconcerting that I moved my chair back before I continued. "I want you to know that having you for a friend has meant a lot to me. Both you and Jenn. Actually, your whole family is a second family to me." It felt right, like I was taking the high road.

He nodded. "Okay," he said, "that's good. But, Kennie . . . you know I'm in love with you, right?"

I shook my head vigorously. I thought we'd cleared this up. I opened my mouth to speak, but he put his hand up to stop me.

"I love you, Kendra. I always will. Anytime you need me to talk, or spy, or anything, just ask." Then he got up, made the universal "call me" sign, and went behind the counter.

I stood abruptly, jostling the table with my legs.

Bo winked at me from behind the counter. "See ya 'round," he said as I walked out the door.

Later, at work, I rehashed memories of Bo and me: his sister Glory babysitting us, watching *The Little Mermaid*, floating boats in the tub. Climbing trees after supper and not coming down until dark. Then I remembered the time we played keep away and I tackled him and made his nose bleed. He cried and Jenn laughed at him, so he ran home and didn't speak to us for days.

The rain sprinkled gently, and the sky was dark. The weather mirrored my life. The summer had barely started, and I'd lost a father to an affair, my best friend to a sketchy boyfriend, and now Bo.

Before heading home I went by the brownstone. The shift in my world had left me feeling uneasy, and spying was like a default. Dad's car was already there and the van in front of it. The rainy night was perfect for seeing in the windows. I did a U-turn at the top of the street and sped to my spot. Or what I thought was my spot.

Where was it? Frantically, I looked around, thinking I'd overshot it. I reviewed my surroundings. There was the apartment, the tiny alley next to it, the hydrant, the oaks in the median strip, and the bigger oak Bo and I had hidden behind.

Someone was in my parking space.

A horn blared and my heart jumped. Behind me, a truck released its brakes with a hiss and was inching its way toward my bumper. I hit the gas and roared ahead.

I parked around the corner and slumped in my seat. If I

wanted to see anything, I'd have to walk in the rain. Instead, I called Mom.

"Hi Mom, do you need me to pick up anything for dinner?"

"Thanks, Kendra, but your dad's taking me out. I hope you can keep yourself busy tonight."

"Oh, no problem." It's a guilt date, but she doesn't know it. "Where are you going?"

"A concert in Portland. One of our old favorites."

"Nice." Perfect. He's dredging up memories from their past.

"Is everything okay?"

"Fine. Love you. Have fun tonight."

I called Dad and he picked up on the first ring.

"Hey," he said.

"Hey, just wanted to say hi. Mom says you guys are going out tonight."

"Oh yeah, a blast from the past. I should probably head out and meet her soon."

"Where are you?"

"I'm at the marina working on the boat."

I pictured him having cocktails in the living room with Skipper.

"Dad?" My mouth went dry as I formed my words.

"Yeah, honey," he said. "You want to join us tonight? Hang with the old folks?"

I got my senses back. "Nope, thanks. I've got a date."

"Another time, then."

I opened the burner phone, selected the photo of Dad and his girlfriend kissing in front of the brownstone. I'd send this one later, when he was at the concert with Mom.

THE TRAFFIC WAS BACKED UP AS USUAL AT THE bridge, but it gave me a view of the Clam Shack and Will's crazy blond hair every time he handed out an order. The place was always packed, even when it wasn't the dinner hour.

I inched my way along and hoped he'd see my car. When I was right beside the shack, he popped out of the door and handed someone an order.

And then it looked like he gave her a kiss and ran back into the booth. A quick kiss, but a kiss.

My breath caught in my throat and I forced myself to swallow.

Horns blared and someone hollered behind me. "Move it!"

I snapped out of it and drove the car length I'd gained.

Was that Nicole? Her back was to me, but it definitely could have been, and that would mean Will was a liar.

While I sat in traffic, I called Jenn. It went right to voice mail, so I left a frantic message about how Will was lying and cheating and we'd barely gotten started. I got through Market Square without a panic attack and sped off toward home.

Was it possible that I was too pissed off to panic?

The light rain that had been a nuisance became a downpour, and I prayed it was ruining Nicole's hair. It was definitely making it hard for me to see the road.

Yelling obscenities and pounding on the steering wheel was my fix for dealing with the rain, Will, and Dad. And for the most part it worked. By the time I pulled into the driveway, I'd decided what to do.

I got out the burner phone and sent the photo to Dad. Then I texted Will.

Me: Was that you kissing Nicole at the Clam Shack?

No. I didn't want to be that whiney girl. Instead, I sent a different text to Will.

Me: I passed you at the Clam Shack today. Miss you already.

Before I'd even gotten into the house, I felt the phone vibrate in my bag. I took it out and looked at the text.

John: Who is this? What do you want?

FOR A LIE FOR A LIE FOR A LIE
LIE FOR A LIE FOR A LIE FOR A LIE
OR A LIE FOR A LIE FOR A LIE
FOR A LIE FOR A LIE FOR A
FOR A LIE FOR A LIE FOR A LIE
LIE FOR A LIE FOR A LIE FOR A LIE FOR
A LIE FOR A LIE FOR A LIE FOR

CHAPTER 16

THE NEXT MORNING I WOKE UP EARLY AND LAY IN bed, thinking about the brownstone and how I had lost my parking spot and didn't get to spy. I sneaked out before anyone was up, got a large coffee, and parked in my spot on the other side of the median. I trained my zoom lens on the window and channeled my inner P.I. As soon as I could, I'd find out this woman's real name. I was pretty sure it wasn't Skipper.

The night before was a deep disappointment; it was totally possible that both Dad *and* Will were cheaters. Damn.

I didn't want Bo to be right, so I was going to be cool until I knew for sure.

After fifteen minutes of no movement, the white cat jumped onto the windowsill and settled on its haunches. Then it leaned in and rubbed against the glass. Shortly afterward somebody patted its head. Was it the woman or the girl? I had my answer when Jilly came out the door and sat on the steps. She had a big canvas bag and a boogie board. Beach day! Then the woman came out and put the key in the planter, and they both got in the van.

I had learned my lesson the time they came back for the mouth guard, so I stayed put until my coffee was gone. A good ten minutes went by, and then I heard a series of beeps from the new phone. I dug through my bag until I found it.

There was a text: *What do you want?*

He sent the same text again. He wanted an answer.

I texted back: *Do the right thing.*

I went across the street and let myself in.

The first thing I did was run up to the bathroom and take a pee. Then I opened Rex's cage. He ran around the cage frantically and then went in his tunnel and hid.

"I'm not trying to pick you up; I'm setting you free. Go!" I said, jiggling the cage a little. He didn't move, but I was pretty sure he'd find his way out later.

Before going back downstairs, I stepped into the master bedroom. I crossed the floor to a window and looked down on the street. My car was visible from here and it made me nervous, even though nobody was home. I'd pick a better spot next time.

The king-size bed took up most of the small room, and

the matching dressers with a head-to-toe mirror in between could mean only one thing: He was at home here.

I opened the drawers and found jewelry and scarves. I took a chunky silver bracelet. In the other dresser were Dad's socks. The drawer below was T-shirts. Below that his button-downs. I turned and opened the closet. Next to her dresses there was a suit and a dress coat. I put my hand in the pocket. Peppermints. My heart sank.

I was halfway down the stairs when I bolted back up and ran to the master bedroom. Something had caught my eye in the jewelry drawer.

I fished through the tangle of scarves and jewelry until I found it. There it was: the little Spanish dancer. I pocketed it and went into Jilly's room. In the cedar box on her dresser was another Spanish dancer necklace and a sailing medal. I took both and went down to the kitchen and turned on the computer.

While it was booting up, I looked through the stuff on the desk. There was the usual assortment of pencils, tape, markers, notepads, and clips. I put a sailboat paperweight in my bag.

Most people have a place where they keep their mail and their junk mail. I know we do. I looked under the desk (where we kept ours), and there it was—a junk mail bucket like at home. I reached in and took a few envelopes. *Current Resident.*

I got on the floor and pulled the bucket out, pawing through it and not caring about the mess I was making. The anger welling up in my gut was barely contained. There were only supermarket flyers and a few empty envelopes. I kicked the mess back under the desk and opened the drawer.

Bingo.

Business cards from Old Port Toyota. Gail Halstrom, Sales.

That's how I know her! Gail and Hal Halstrom. They were our old friends from the boat trip. My mind spun through those weekends on the *Calliope*. I remembered Gail as a sweet lady with a long red ponytail.

Now I understood our stare-down on the sidewalk. Even with her sunglasses and shorter hair. Even though we both looked completely different. We had experienced a trauma together that was imprinted on us forever.

And we recognized each other.

How long has this affair been going on?

On my way out the door, I grabbed two candlesticks off the mantel. I ran across the street to my car, but before hopping in, I went to the rear bumper to see something I knew would be there: a sticker from Old Port Toyota.

It was Sunday, so nobody would be at the law office. I could go through the photo album again. On the way, I felt the outline of the Spanish dancers in my pocket.

Dad had been on to a trip to Spain for a conference; because it was work-related, Mom and I couldn't go. When I cried and wouldn't let go of him, he promised to bring us presents. And he did. He brought Mom and me each a necklace with a beautiful dancer on the end. Mine with blond hair and Mom's with dark. The ones in my pocket had red and blond.

The office was empty and quiet except for the bubbling coming from Bubba's tank. I sat at Uncle Steve's desk, got the album from the drawer, and flipped to the photos of the boat trip day.

And there she was, happy and laughing between Hal and Dad. Sitting on the bow, sunbathing with Mom and me. And one of her on the dock, holding Hal's hand. Gail Halstrom and Dad.

When my phone rang, I wasn't surprised when I saw Dad's number. I knew it was coming.

"Yeah, Dad," I said, bracing myself for being found out.

"It's about Grandma. Please come home now."

———————

THE HOUSE WAS QUIET, AND MOM AND DAD WERE at the kitchen table. Mom's eyes were puffy, and Dad was slouching in his chair.

"Honey," Dad said, "Grandma died last night. They think it was a heart attack."

"But I just talked to her," I said, sitting down across from him.

"She's had a condition for some time, but I didn't think . . . I thought she'd live forever." Dad laughed softly.

Mom put her arm around me and squeezed.

Dad cleared his throat. "The funeral is in Massachusetts. We'll go down in the morning."

For a moment all was forgotten as we cried together and then later at dinner sat with Uncle Steve and Aunt Mimi and talked about Grandma. We remembered the way she'd held us together when we came back from the accident. She was all business and sweet calmness.

By the end of dinner the funeral was planned, and the shock was beginning to wear off. That's when Gail Halstrom and Dad popped into my mind, and piggybacking on that horrid discovery was the image of Will and Nicole at the Clam Shack.

Before this day of death and discoveries, I might not have had the courage to confront Will, but now I was eager to hear what he had to say. I texted him to meet me at the island.

I emptied the brownstone goodies in my closet, put my camera in my bag, and on my way out took a magnum of champagne from the liquor cabinet.

Will's car was already there, and so were Doug's and Bo's. Jenn came rushing up and threw her arms around me.

"I'm so sorry about your grandma. She was awesome." She hugged me again.

"Can you come with me to the funeral? It's in Massachusetts. There's no way I can deal with Dad for that long. Alone."

She raised an eyebrow. "His mother just died. Give him a break."

"That's not why. I just want—" I shook my head. "Forget it," I said, walking off to find Will. He was at the fire, feeding it with pieces of cardboard.

"Hey," I said.

"Hey," he said back.

"Want to share this with me?" I said, opening my bag to show him the champagne.

"A magnum. That's a bottle for each of us," he said.

I followed him to the back side of the island where the dunes dropped off steeply. We skidded down the sandy slope to where it leveled off, and sat with our backs against a rock. His mouth was on mine before I could take a breath, but it didn't matter. His breath was my breath; my breath was his breath.

And then I remembered. I pushed him off and asked him, "Are you still seeing Nicole?"

He laughed. "No, I told you we're just friends. Friends do

things. Like talk." He nuzzled my neck and reached under my shirt.

"When I passed the Clam Shack today, I thought I saw you kiss her," I said while he continued to nibble.

"She was there with Sam and Dory." His nibble turned into a gentle suck, and then it became more intense.

"I don't like you seeing her," I said, knowing I sounded as if I were in middle school.

"I don't like seeing her, either. I like seeing you," he said, moving to my mouth and kissing me deeply. "I like you more than anyone."

I stopped pushing his hand away and lay down. I pulled his shirt up so I could run my hands up and down his muscles. He felt as warm and smooth as I remembered. Soon his teeth were back in the crook of my shoulder and neck. It was a magic spot and he'd shown it to me. I rolled over and did the same to him.

"Kendra," he said softly, "you look amazing. Where have you been hiding so long?"

I giggled a little and leaned over enough to let my hair fall into his face. "I wasn't hiding. You just forgot." I kissed his chest and belly.

Gathering my hair into a ponytail, he said, "Sometimes you're behind that camera too much," he said.

I got off him and reached for the champagne. Aiming it

straight toward the open ocean, I uncorked it, and a log plume of foam erupted. We mouthed the bottle together, laughing as we lapped up the drips. Then he held it while I drank a long swallow. I'd had it before at weddings, but never so much, and never so fast. I held some in my mouth and let the bubbles tickle my tongue. It was a big bottle, and we passed it back and forth like soda, alternating between kisses and gulps.

I lay back and felt the whoosh of the alcohol.

"Where'd you get this?" he asked.

"Dad."

"Nice of him."

"It was, wasn't it?"

"A car and champagne. What did you do to deserve this?"

"It's not what *I* did; it's what *he* did."

"Oh," he said, nodding like he understood, which scared me for a second, so I drank some more. And then it hit like I was realizing it for the first time again.

"Did you hear me? It's not what I did, it's what he did." This made me erupt into howls of laughter, which made me laugh harder for laughing at something so terrible.

We moved to where the rocks trailed into the water, and drank more of the champagne. My head sloshed inside as I turned toward Will. I was feeling so much at once, and it was all mixed together, the good and the bad, the beautiful and the horrible. Looking at Will was the beautiful part. I rested against the crook of his shoulder and hugged the bottle. Then he grabbed it from me and held it up toward the darkening sky.

"To John."

I shook my head.

"It's a toast. Thanks for the drinks. I'll get the next round," he said, waving the bottle at the water.

"Oh, right," I said.

"Your dad's cool, Kendra." He put the bottle to my lips and I sipped. "One time he picked me up hitchhiking, and get this: I know he knew I was drunk, but he never told my parents."

"What a guy," I said. My eyes closed on their own and I sighed. "Did you know my grandmother died?"

He laid me down again, and this time a rock jabbed hard into my spine. I cried out, but he just moaned, kissing me hard and feeling my breasts. I arched my back to get off the rock. "Yeah, Kennie, just like that."

I wriggled. "No, I need to—"

"Here," he said, holding the bottle to my mouth.

I got onto my elbow and swigged. "Did you know that our parents used to party here?"

He drank and nodded. "Yeah, I think your mom and my dad went out together."

"Can you believe it?" I said, shaking my head and liking the feeling inside.

"But your mom dumped my dad," he said.

"Big mistake. But look at us; we're meant to be." I stood up, then caught myself before I fell. "Gotta pee."

"Hurry back," he said.

My body was headed in the right direction, but my head was doing something different. "Where's Jenn?" I wanted to tell her everything. I stumbled a few steps. "Jenn!" I made it to the path and climbed up a little, then fell onto my ass. "Jenn!"

Will appeared, laughing, and helped me the rest of the way. "You are so smashed," he said, heading me off to the bushes. In the distance I could see the fire circle glowing and everyone milling around.

"There's no way I'm peeing over there. No way." I reached for my bag, but it wasn't across my shoulder. Gone. My camera. Gone. A panic rose quickly. "Go get Jenn, please. Please, Will. I only pee with Jenn."

"Is this the first time you've been drunk?"

I opened my mouth and then shut it quickly so I could think about how I should answer. But I couldn't think. The island swirled around me, and I reached blindly for something, anything. "Where is my camera?" I wanted to be looking through the lens right then. Everything would be clear if I could see through the lens.

Will plunked me down. "Sit here."

"No, don't go," I said, grabbing his shirttail.

He wrenched himself free. "I thought you wanted me to get Jenn."

"And my camera. I need my camera." I looked down at the dune where we'd been making out and touched my lips, but I couldn't feel them—they were numb, like my forehead. A bubble of laughter came up from my belly. And then the tears came as I thought about my missing camera and Grandma. And Dad.

I rested my head on my arms and closed my eyes while the world spun away into darkness.

Someone shook me.

My eyes searched randomly for the voice while arms lifted me to standing. Jenn? Finally I focused on someone who wasn't Jenn. Or Will. Someone bigger.

It was Bo.

FOR A LIE FOR A LIE FOR A LIE
LIE FOR A LIE FOR A LIE FOR A LIE FOR A LIE FOR A LIE
FOR A LIE FOR A LIE FOR A
LIE FOR A LIE FOR A LIE FOR A
FOR A LIE FOR A LIE FOR A LIE
LIE FOR A LIE FOR A LIE FOR A LIE FOR

A LIE FOR A LIE FOR A LIE FOR
FOR A LIE FOR A LIE FOR A LIE

CHAPTER 17

SLIVERS OF LIGHT STABBED MY EYES, AND MY HEAD hammered with a thousand shouts of protest. I focused on stilling my body and willing my stomach to keep down whatever was left in there. I didn't think it was possible to throw up any more than I already had.

And then I remembered that Grandma was gone, and my body rebelled again. I didn't remember putting the wastebasket beside my bed, but I was glad it was there.

And how'd I get home? I went to the window, which was a bad idea, because my legs weren't getting the message from my very sick brain. I fell on the way, skinning my knees on the rug and banging my elbows. But thankfully I saw what I wanted to see: My car was in the driveway, and Dad's Saab right behind it. They came home after me.

So how did I get here? Poison rose up in my stomach again, and I ran for the wastebasket.

Shivering in my clammy skin, I stepped into a steamy shower. While the water pounded on my aching head, I tried to piece the night together. Soap stung my back where I had scraped it against the rocks. I remembered that. Oh, how I remembered Will's mouth clamped onto the crook of my neck. I shivered again despite the burn of the spray. But I didn't remember driving, so how had I gotten home?

When the sticky, sweet sweat was washed off my skin, I felt halfway human again, but I glimpsed my face in the mirror. My look said it all: *Kendra, you and champagne are not friends. Will never be friends.* I brushed my teeth and swished around some mouthwash, put on some makeup, and went down to the kitchen.

My bag and my camera were plopped in the middle of the kitchen table. I sent a silent thank-you to Bo and called Jenn.

"What happened last night?" I asked her on the phone.

The response was laughter with Doug. Speaking to him she said, "She wants to know what happened last night." Mumbling from Doug.

I held my stomach. "Talk to me, Jenn."

"You want the short version or long?"

"Oh my god, Jenn, just tell me!" I sat at the kitchen table

with a glass of juice, not ready to let it pass my lips, but so thirsty.

"I don't really know all of it because Doug and I were MIA ourselves for a while, but what I heard was that you and Will killed a magnum of champagne. He came back and you didn't."

"I didn't drive, did I?"

"No. Bo drove you in your car, and Sam followed in Bo's truck, and guess what? He and Dory are going out now."

My stomach clenched. "Bo and Dory?" I remembered him helping me up.

"No, Sam. Sam and Dory are going out."

"I didn't drive; I think I can breathe now."

"You were pretty funny, Kendra."

"Pretty disgusting." I sighed loudly. "Jenn, I don't know—"

"What?"

"I can't remember if I—" I couldn't say it.

"You can't remember what you did last night? With Will?"

"I'm freaking out." I sat back down. "Did anyone say anything after I left? Did you talk to Will?"

"I saw Bo talking to him, but that was all. Stop obsessing. Will thought the whole thing was funny."

"I think I'm going to be sick again."

"Next time, eat before you drink, and pace yourself."

"There won't be a next time. I feel like shit. At least Mom and Dad don't know."

The sound of a glass clinking made me jump. I'd spoken too soon. It was Dad at the sink. He turned on the tap.

"Hey, Kennie."

I nodded a little.

"Gotta go," I told Jenn. "We're heading to Grandma's house. Please come with me?"

"Sorry. Can't. Doug and I are going to a reunion for his family. It's in New Jersey, so I'll be gone a week."

"Your mother is letting you go for a week?"

"She's been on the phone with his mother and laid down the Costello Sleepaway Law."

"Which is?"

"Separate bedrooms until you're engaged."

Jenn's going to a family thing with Doug? And when did she learn how to hold her alcohol? This was the stuff we always talked about before it happened, not after.

It was a new reality; Doug was her best friend now.

"I miss you, Jenn."

"I'm not even gone yet." *Oh, yes, you are*, I thought as I said good-bye.

My thoughts of Jenn and Doug at a family reunion were interrupted by Dad's whistling as he filled the dishwasher.

"How are you doing?" he asked me.

"What do you mean?" I said, not knowing where this was going. *Does he know I'm hungover?*

"You just lost your grandmother." He rinsed the glass and put it in the top rack.

"Oh, fine. It's sad. How are you?"

He gave me a long look. "Kendra, don't be surprised if this brings up some old patterns."

"What are you talking about?" *Patterns? You're the one with the patterns*, I thought.

"Your anxiety attacks."

How could he say that? "I'm good. They're gone now."

I looked away but felt him still staring.

"Pack up; we have to head down for the funeral."

Upstairs, I re-sent the photo of Dad and Gail kissing in front of the brownstone to Dad's phone.

Then I texted Will.

Me: Can you forget about last night? On my way to funeral. Be back in a few days.

I sent the same one to Bo, but added: *Thank you.*

⁕

GRANDMA'S HOUSE IN MASSACHUSETTS WAS FILLED with casseroles and visitors. Mom and Aunt Mimi were running around setting things out and putting things away and introducing people, and Dad and Uncle Steve were hanging with relatives and old friends, remembering the good times, I guess. I found myself clinging to the wainscoting and wallpaper. I wanted to be invisible, but there was always the inevitable "You're Kendra, Elsa's only girl grandchild. She loved you so."

Since I hadn't heard back from Will, I sneaked upstairs to make a phone call, but it went to voice mail. I hung up instead of leaving a message. Habit made me dial Jenn, but then I hung up when I remembered that she'd left for New Jersey. Bo immediately popped into my head. He probably hated me now and wouldn't answer. When I couldn't stand it any longer, I called him. No answer.

It went like that all day: me worrying what Will thought about me, and then wondering why Bo wouldn't pick up, and then wishing I could talk about it with Jenn, and then checking my phone again, hoping to hear from somebody.

The next day the crowd thinned out and it was just immediate family that stayed to pack away Grandma's house. What began as polite and practical decision making dissolved into flat-out arguments about family mementos, and finally ended in drunken touch football in the yard.

"I've seen this before," Mimi said, sipping her chardonnay.

Mom joined us at the sliding glass door. "Mmm, yes, déjà

vu all over again." She blew out a breath and flopped into a chair. "Well, I guess all we can do is wait it out."

"What? What's going on?" I asked. Mom and Mimi exchanged a look.

"Your mom and I have seen one too many arguments start during the devil's trifecta: brothers, football, and drinking."

"And then throw their mother's funeral into the mix. Oh my god," my mother said, rubbing her forehead. "Let's just hope they keep their heads."

We heard a faint "Asshole!" come from out back.

"Want to see what kinds of desserts we have?" Mimi said.

The three of us raced one another to the kitchen and loaded our plates with cheesecake, cookies, mini pies, and other gooey offerings. We sat in the living room groaning in pleasure, sharing wordless bites, all the while keeping tabs on the game.

Then Aunt Mimi stood and put her hand on her hip and shook her head.

"What is it?" Mom asked.

"Steve and John are into it. It's started."

Dad and Uncle Steve were standing in the middle of the lawn. Dad had the ball under his arm and was waving his other arm around.

"It's none of your goddamned business, Steven!"

"Think about what you're doing for—" Uncle Steve tried to talk, but he had to keep stopping because Dad was yelling so much. I ran to the kitchen and got my camera. I don't think this is what Mom and Dad meant when they asked me to document the extended-family gathering. I snapped a picture just as Dad yelled, "But I'm not doing anything wrong!"

When I got back, Uncle Steve was looking at the ground and his face was red, and with one final burst he pointed his finger and gritted his teeth and said a few choice words. Dad threw down the ball in a way that reminded me of Jilly and her life jacket.

Snapshot.

"Let's do the dishes," Mom said. She scooped up some dirty plates; Mimi did the same, and I followed suit. In the kitchen the dishwasher was already roaring, so we put them in the sink.

"Do you think they'd notice if we went to bed?" Mimi asked.

"Probably not," Mom said. They both laughed at this.

"Do you think they'd notice if we went out?" Mimi asked.

"No driving," I said, trying to sound gruff.

They giggled like two teenagers and hung up their aprons. Definitely the wine talking. I picked up Mom's dishrag and dried while she and Aunt Mimi bonded with the wine. It was nice to see Mom laughing, but I suddenly felt sad. Here I was in Grandma's house, feeling her presence everywhere, smelling the special Grandma smell, a blend of lavender and mothballs—which doesn't sound nice, but it is—and she was gone. I felt her, but she was gone.

I was worried about forgetting her, and her thick white hair and blue eyes. What if the memories of her driving me to school and walking me to my classroom were forgotten? She didn't just do it as a chore for Mom and Dad; she sat in the back of the classroom when I could barely make it through the day.

And her cup custard. I'd never have that again.

I spent the rest of the night by the pool with my feet in the water while I jotted down moments and recipes I never wanted to forget.

In the morning it was Uncle Steve and Aunt Mimi and Mom and Dad by the pool, but I was the only one actually eating breakfast.

"What time is the funeral?" I asked.

Dad cleared his throat and took a sip of juice. "One o'clock," he said. "We have the service at the church and then the burial at the Sullivan plot for immediate family only."

I noticed that Uncle Steve was tearing his bacon into tiny pieces. He stopped when he felt my stare and winked at me.

Later, when I was putting our bags in the trunk of the car, he came up behind me and gave my ponytail a tug.

"This sort of thing is loaded, you know?" he said, taking one of the bags from me.

"Loaded?" I had an idea he was referring to the football game.

"Your dad and I have a lot of history in this house, and your grandmother was a big part of it." He shuffled his feet on the gravel driveway.

"Of course," I said.

"He's complicated. He's smart, tough. He does what he thinks is right, and he's really a good man. He never intends to hurt anyone."

My body froze, but my words flew out. "Are you trying to tell me something?"

"No, but your dad is—"

I slammed the trunk shut. "I know. He's complicated. That's not an excuse for bad behavior."

Now we both froze. I had said too much. When I looked up, I saw compassion in Uncle Steve's eyes. He opened up his arms and I fell into them.

"Look, Kendra," he said, holding me tightly, "whatever your dad's done, I think you should give him a chance to explain."

I pulled back and looked at him. "You know about Gail Halstrom, don't you?"

He seemed relieved.

"We were in an impossible situation." He shook his head and paced in a small circle.

"*We?* Mimi knew, too? Does Mom know?"

"I'm so sorry, Kendra," he said, reaching for me.

"Stop." I opened the car door, then changed my mind and started back toward the house, but Dad, Mom, and Mimi were coming down the walk. I looked at Uncle Steve. "Don't tell *anyone* I know. This is one secret you *should* keep."

"This is so sad," Mimi said. "Too soon." She dabbed at her eyes as she headed to her car with Uncle Steve.

Dad put his arms around my shoulders. "I'm coming back here after the burial, and you and Mom are going back to Maine. I have a lot to straighten out here at the house." He kissed the top of my head and held the car door for me.

I looked back at Grandma's house and imagined her waving from the doorway. I closed my eyes and took a snapshot with my mind.

FOR A LIE FOR A LIE FOR A LIE FOR A LIE FOR A L
FOR A LIE FOR A LIE FOR A LIE FOR A LIE FOR A LIE
IE FOR A LIE FOR A LIE FOR A LIE FOR A LIE FOR A LIE
R A LIE FOR A LIE FOR A LIE FOR A LIE FO
FOR A LIE FOR A LIE FOR A LIE FOR A
R A LIE FOR A LIE FOR A LIE FOR A LIE FOR A LIE
EFOR A LIE FOR A LIE FOR A LIE FOR A LIE FOR A

CHAPTER 18

IT WAS A RELIEF TO CROSS THE BORDER AND HAVE Grandma's funeral behind me. And I wasn't disappointed Dad was staying behind. *Welcome to Maine, The Way Life Should Be.* Even though I'd always made fun of it before, I was happy to see the familiar sign. Soon I could smell the ocean, and the speeding traffic slowed as we drove past the beaches. In Kingsport the seawall was packed with tourists and sunbathers, beach umbrellas, and babies in carriages. Every once in a while I'd get a whiff of sunscreen and hear the yelp of a kid or a mom hollering. It all seemed so normal. Even Mom looked more comfortable now that we were back here. Tapping her manicured fingernail on the steering wheel, she sang along with the radio, and I didn't make fun of her.

Once we were in our driveway, Mom put the car in park and we threw our arms around each other in a silent hug. Grandma was gone. No words were necessary.

Mom went into the house, but I stayed outside and texted Bo. From the driveway I could see his truck parked in his driveway.

Me: Did you see my call?

I got the bags from the trunk and my phone beeped.

Bo: Yes
Me: Yes, but you aren't going to call back?
Bo: Correct

I dumped the bags in the upstairs hall and flopped on my bed with my arms over my eyes. I got why Bo was done with me, but what was going on with Will?

I got my answer when I drove to the beach. Will was leaning into Nicole's driver-side window. Were they just talking? Were they kissing?

They're just friends, Kendra.

A car horn blared, and I looked up in time to slam on my brakes. My heart beat in my throat as I pulled over to the sidewalk and parked. I looked back, and Will and Nicole were watching me. He said something to her and crossed the street to my car.

"You're back," he said, leaning in to kiss me.

Relief poured over me, and I wrapped my arms around his neck and pulled him into the car. "Get in here."

"Okay, okay, let me go," he said, extracting himself from my grip.

He ran around the front of my car, surfer hair blowing around his laughing face. I'd been worried for nothing.

"I thought you were going to kill someone," he said, nodding toward the traffic.

"Yeah, I guess I wasn't paying attention. It's been a hard few days."

He leaned into my neck and moaned. "I've missed the smell of your hair."

I turned my head, hoping Nicole saw him smelling my hair, but she was gone. "I missed you, too," I said, pulling him close.

"Are you coming out tonight?" he asked, reaching under my shirt.

"Definitely." I moved his hand to my back and tried to distract him with a kiss, but his hand crept under my shirt again.

When I moved it away a second time, he said, "I've gotta be at work." He fished in his pocket and got his keys.

"Tonight," I said, reaching through the window and squeezing his hand.

"See if you can get more champagne," he said.

I CONTINUED AROUND THE BEACH LOOP. THE island was a silhouette against the late-June sunset. I sent Mom a text, telling her I was going to the movies. She replied that she was going to bed early anyway.

I drove to Portland with my mind set on going to the brownstone if it looked empty. I drove with the music as loud as I could take it, ignoring the phone calls and texts that lit up my phone. The air was humid and heavy, so I closed the windows and turned on the AC and let my forehead cool. I parked and watched the windows for light or movement.

After fifteen minutes of nothing happening, I went across the street and looked into the darkened room. Only the cat was home, so I let myself in. The foyer felt echoey and cold. I stood motionless for a few seconds and waited for movement from any direction, but nothing came.

I turned on the flashlight app on my phone and set the timer for ten minutes. Upstairs, Jilly's room was still messy and Rex's cage was still open. I peeked in, but no Rex. Ha! Mission accomplished.

I was curious about Gail. I went back to the master bedroom. The same book was on Gail's bedside table next to some eyeglasses, but the photo I'd broken was now gone. On Dad's side was a photo of the *Calliope*. We had the same one at home. I took it and the eyeglasses.

I went down to the living room and took the photo of the three of them off the piano and put it in my bag. Then I grabbed up a great blue heron figurine from a side table, and from the computer desk between the living room and kitchen, a silver letter opener with an ivory handle. When I heard the door open, I put it all in my bag and slipped into the broom closet.

Through the louvered door I heard Jilly say, "I'm gonna go play Skate Craze on my iPad."

"Nope, dinner first," Gail said. Jilly ran upstairs anyway.

Then my heart banged in my chest as I heard Dad's familiar steps coming toward the closet. He passed the doors and sat in front of the computer. I alternated between feeling pissed off and scared of being caught breaking and entering. And having stolen goods on me, too.

I settled on pissed off. Bullshit he was in Massachusetts taking care of the house.

Jilly called down the stairs. "Can I have hot dogs for supper?" she asked.

"I'm good with that. You, John?" Gail asked.

"I'm not hungry," he said.

There was the sound of unpacking a grocery bag on the

counter, and then the fridge door opening. I watched through the slats as Dad pushed his chair back and went to the kitchen.

"Thanks for coming down, it meant a lot to me," he said. "Mom would have loved you." I couldn't see, but I imagined them hugging each other tightly and then kissing. I dug my nails into my palms.

Jilly walked into the room and stood in front of the louvered doors. "Gross, you guys."

"Hey, champ, hugs are a good thing," Dad said. "Better watch out or you're gonna get one!" Two bodies flew past the door, a little one and a big one. Jilly yelled for help, and Dad pretended to be a monster. I knew this game. It was my game, my dad, and my nickname. *Champ* belonged to me.

They ran back into the kitchen, laughing and squealing as he caught her. Then the squeal turned into a piercing scream.

It's over, I thought.

The three of them huddled on the floor just past the computer table.

"Rex! Rex!" Jilly cried.

Gail and Dad tried to calm Jilly while she screamed and cried.

I squinted through the door, but I couldn't see anything.

"I'll get the dustpan," said Gail.

Dustpan! Shit! I pushed harder into the corner and steadied my heavy bag of trinkets.

"No, I got it," Dad said. I could hear newspapers rustling and remembered the junk mail bucket under the desk.

"How come he's only got a face and tail?" she sobbed. "Where's the rest of him?"

"I think Sonar ate Rex."

My hand went silently to my mouth.

Jilly began her heaving sobs again.

"You probably forgot to close his cage. I'm sorry, champ," Dad said.

I had only wanted Rex to run around and poop everywhere. My heart raced, and beads of sweat popped out on my forehead and under my armpits.

Dad rubbed Jilly's back. "Mistakes happen."

Through the slats I could see Dad's and Jilly's shoes only three feet from the broom closet. I was trapped.

"But I didn't leave the cage open. I really didn't, Daddy."

Daddy?

CHAPTER 19

JILLY CALLED HIM DADDY AND ACTED LIKE THAT was normal. Rage flooded me, and images flashed through my mind: the crinkles at the edges of her eyes, her mouth when she laughed, the way she stiffened her shoulders when she got mad, her walk. She had Dad's face.

Of course she was his kid.

Dad's phone rang, and I put my hand to my pocket automatically and turned mine off.

Listening to him talk to someone was so weird. Nothing was unusual for him, but all I could think of was Jilly saying "Daddy."

I tilted my head to see out the slats of the door. Dad was fiddling with the computer and talking quietly on the phone. And then, after a long sigh, he said loudly, "I know, I know."

He continued to click away at the computer. I strained to see, but it was only a stripy image of the floor.

Then he left the room and called up the stairs. "I have to take care of something—be back in an hour."

The front door shut. The only sounds were pattering footsteps upstairs, so I cracked the closet door and listened.

After a few minutes it was clear that Gail and Jilly were settled upstairs. I stepped quietly into the living room. The theme song from Skate Craze was playing, and an irritated Gail was arguing on the phone.

"I don't care about that, John. I know what I know. Someone was in here."

I stopped in the foyer, hand on the doorknob, and listened.

"Exactly," she said, like they were agreeing on something. She padded across the master bedroom and back again. And then stopped. "Don't you think we should deal with this together?" she cried as her footsteps thumped into the hall and down the stairs. "I'll call you back."

I bolted before she saw me, slammed the front door, and ran in the shadows all the way to the car. As I drove away, I glanced down the road and saw Gail standing in the light of the doorway, looking out into the street.

I wanted to text Bo and tell him everything, but I knew I couldn't. I drove straight to the island.

I pulled over and brought up the pictures on the burner phone. I selected one of the Asian art masks.

Me: Do the right thing.

I almost added *asshole* to it, but didn't. Before I was back on the road, he responded.

John: I am.

What a bastard. How dare he?

I parked next to Will. The only other cars were Dory's, Sam's, and Nicole's. I barely thought about the tide, just enough to dodge the pools of water. What I needed was to talk about my dad, my mom, and now Jilly.

Shit, I had a half sister.

The fire was low, and it was oddly quiet when I walked up to the small circle of four.

"Hey," I said.

"Hey," Will said.

Dory, Sam, and Nicole got up and walked by me toward the causeway.

"Call me later, Will," Sam said.

Will grunted an acknowledgement.

"I can clear a room, I guess," I said, sitting next to him.

I dropped my bag, keenly aware of its rattling contents. "I have to tell you something," I said, and began to cry.

"Hey." He pulled me close, hugging me tightly. "It can't be that bad." He held me at arm's length and smiled his gorgeous crooked smile. The light from the fire made his skin a warmer bronze than usual.

Just as I opened my mouth to tell him everything, he kissed me. For a minute I wanted to just do that, kiss Will and forget about what had happened, but I couldn't. I pulled away and told him about Dad having a girlfriend and a daughter and that I had to tell Mom and I didn't want to, and how it was even more complicated by Jilly, who was my half sister.

I told him I was really scared.

Will squeezed my shoulder while I cried. "It can't be that bad," he said again. And he squeezed my shoulder some more.

"Thanks for listening. It's all I could think about while I was hiding in the dark. I just wanted someone to talk to." I dug in my bag and found a tissue. "Now that we have a real relationship, we can do that for each other."

Will grabbed a stick and poked the fire to life.

"I mean, we can be there for each other," I said, searching his face for some recognition of emotion. "I mean, now that you don't see Nicole . . ."

He walked over to the pile of driftwood, picked up a couple of sticks, and threw them on the fire. Sparks crackled and floated into the night sky.

He stood with his back to me, stirring the fire, oddly silent.

"Hey, come here," I said from my perch on the log behind him. I tugged on his shorts.

He came and sat beside me, and I kissed him with all the meaning I could. I wanted him to get that I was just temporarily upset, that I wouldn't always be a crying mess. I kissed him in a way that would let him know I was a party girl, too, but I was never going to party as hard as I did the night we drank the champagne. And somewhere between my kisses and mumblings, I wanted him to feel like we were best friends and that I would be there for him when he needed to unload.

"And I want to say thanks for cutting it off with Nicole."

He pulled back and looked away.

"I mean, I know you hang out. Like close friends," I said.

"You're talking like you think I did something wrong, but you don't really want to say it," he said, still not looking at me.

I sighed loudly. "It's been so crazy lately, and everything's mixed up. I'm sorry, Will," I said, trying to backtrack.

"We're not exclusive." He whipped his stick into the fire and immediately got up, found another one, and sat back down.

"Exactly!" That's what I'd been waiting for and what I had needed to hear all along. "Whew, that's a relief," I said, leaning into him and rubbing his back.

"No, Kendra, *we're* not exclusive." He motioned between us with his stick.

My stomach clenched, and the patch of sand in front of me blurred. I let the feeling pass through me and vowed not to cry about this. I stood up and slung my bag over my shoulder and stomped to the rock steps.

"Are you mad?" he asked. I turned, but he didn't wait for me to answer. "I didn't do anything wrong."

"No, not really wrong," I said. "I was crazy to think this was going to be something. You gave me every sign that you're a complete asshole, and I pretended it wasn't happening." Will was just like my father.

He stepped back like I'd punched him.

"No, really, Will. How many times did you fool around with Nicole while we were together?"

He scrunched his face like he was searching for the answer to an unsolvable math problem. "I told you, we weren't exclusive."

"We're not anything now."

I LEFT HIM RIGHT THERE AND WADED THROUGH THE rising tide alone, using the flashlight on my phone to guide me. Stumbling over rocks and getting tangled in the floating seaweed, I had one thought: not that the water was going to pull me under, not that I was going to drown, but that from here on I wasn't going to have any secrets or tell any lies.

And that included how I felt about Bo.

FOR A LIE FOR A LIE FOR A LIE
FOR A LIE FOR A LIE FOR A LIE FOR A LIE
FOR A LIE FOR A LIE FOR A LIE
FOR A LIE FOR A LIE
FOR A LIE FOR A LIE FOR A LIE FOR A LIE
FOR A LIE FOR A LIE FOR A LIE FOR A LIE FOR A
FOR A LIE FOR A LIE FOR

CHAPTER 20

I WOKE UP KNOWING THAT IT WAS THE DAY I'D SHUT down Operation Snapshot. That meant taking everything back to the brownstone. Jilly had her regular Sunday soccer game at one o'clock, and this one was in Wells, about forty-five minutes away.

Mom and Dad were at a golf tournament luncheon, so I parked in my spot and waited for the blue van to leave. When it did, I waited another five minutes before I let myself in.

What I was doing would make it right. I had everything with me, and it was all going back.

I couldn't replace Rex, though, and I felt terrible.

I set the great blue heron back on the side table, the photos on the baby grand, and the candlesticks on the mantel. I sat at the computer and put the letter opener where I'd found it and the sailboat paperweight on top of some papers.

Everything looked the way it should downstairs.

I moved upstairs, quickly returning the Spanish dancer necklace to Gail's jewelry drawer with the chunky silver bracelet. I put the photo of the *Calliope* back on Dad's bedside table and returned Gail's glasses.

Jilly's room was total chaos as usual, and Rex's cage was still in the corner. I opened her cedar box and put the Spanish dancer back, along with the sailing medal.

I raced downstairs and out the door, feeling immediately lighter. Not completely weightless, but lighter. I could check that off my list of Things to Put Right.

Next was Bo. I sent him a text.

Me: Operation Snapshot spun out of control. I just shut it down.

I headed for the café in the hope that he'd want to see me. My phone beeped, and I pulled over to check it.

Bo: If you want to debrief be at the café at 5:30.

Relief flooded me. There was a chance that Bo didn't totally hate me. And if he did, I was determined to fix it.

I GOT THERE ON TIME, BUT THE LIGHTS WERE OFF and the chairs were flipped up on the tables. He could've changed his mind about meeting me, and if he did, I couldn't blame him. I'd yanked him around enough. But I took a chance he was around back.

The picnic table was set with two smoothies and a big, fat candle, and Bo was sitting on top, waiting.

"I heard," he said.

"What did you hear?" I said, a million things going through my mind.

"You dumped Will on his ass," he said.

I stopped, halfway there, and caught my breath. Was Bo pissed? If he was, I wouldn't be surprised. I'd cast him aside for a complete loser. Now I was going forward, new and clean and fresh, and with total honesty. No matter what happened from this step forward, I was going to be real.

"I dumped him on Beach Rose Island," I said. "He didn't expect it, but I'm pretty sure he was over it before he got across the causeway."

He laughed and patted the picnic table. "Have a drink," he said. I settled beside him and sipped the smoothie.

"Mmm, peanut butter and banana," I said.

"Your favorite."

"So good," I said, trying to swallow. There was a lump in

my throat. I jumped off the table and shook out my hands and stomped my feet a little.

"You okay?" Bo asked. He started to get down off the table, but I put up my hand.

"Yeah," I said, tears pooling in my eyes. I wiped them away. *This is it*, I thought. *This is what love is. Someone forgives you for pushing them away and then when you want them back, they make you your favorite smoothie.*

It was that simple.

I planted myself between his thighs and hugged him around the waist. Looking up at him, I said, "I'm so sorry I hurt you." And I meant it. I filled him in on all my sleuthing, all my criminal activity, and everything I did to make it right again.

I waited, face tilted up at him, eyes open and heart open, too, for him to kiss me, but it didn't come. Instead, he moved off the table and lifted me onto it. He took my face between his giant hands and held it. Then he kissed me. It would have been the perfect ending to a tough day.

And then I got a text.

Dad: Meet me at the house. Now.

CHAPTER 21

I WALKED INTO THE KITCHEN AND FOUND DAD alone at the table. It wasn't unlike the night we found out Grandma had died.

Expressionless, he motioned for me to sit.

"Where's Mom?" I asked.

"She'll be back later," he said. "Right now it's just you and me and this," he said, turning his laptop around for me to see.

I gasped and covered my mouth. It was me, on video, in the brownstone; me in the kitchen opening the fridge, me in the bedroom by the dresser, me at the baby grand with my bag fat with stuff I'd stolen. There were multiple views that looped over and over. And one showed fear on my face as I ran toward the broom closet.

I looked at Dad and opened my mouth to speak, but I could only manage a squeak. The panic that I'd conquered was back. I stood up quickly, knocking my chair to the floor, and ran to the sink and turned on the faucet. I needed water. And air—I wanted air. Pins of light floated in front of my eyes, and my throat tightened. *One breath*, I thought. If I could get one breath . . . I stuck my head out the door and forced myself to breathe.

Behind me the water still ran in the sink. Dad got up and turned it off.

"Kendra, count to ten."

I froze. That's how he used to help me when I was little.

"I can do it myself," I said. "Asshole." I shut the door but didn't turn around.

I heard him sit back down. "Of course you can. And I am an asshole."

He'd left a glass of water by the sink and I downed it.

"Please sit so we can talk, Kennie."

I did, but I shut the laptop first.

He set his phone on the table, opened to my text and photo. *Do the right thing.*

All I could do was shake my head. I didn't know where to start. Then it hit me. There was also video of me today, *putting back* what I'd taken. I was doing the right thing. He was the one who needed to explain himself.

"I thought it might be you," he said.

"Really?"

"Well I couldn't be sure. I needed proof." He let out a loud sigh. "My God, Ken, stealing?" He shook his head.

I raised my eyebrows at him. "Don't try to be the good parent now. You're the one who needs to explain himself."

He looked away for a few seconds and then nodded. "Okay. It started after the accident. I always felt like Hal was killed because of me. I still do. So I helped Gail get back on her feet after Hal's death. She didn't know how to deal with his business."

"Jesus, Dad," I said, "what about helping us? We were a mess. And Mom's leg . . ."

"I couldn't have survived without Grandma," he said, his voice catching.

I wondered if she'd suspected. "Did she know about you and Gail?"

"She asked me if I was having an affair. We argued, but I denied it. Ever since, there's been tension."

"I called her, you know, and told her," I said.

His head shot up, like he was surprised, but then he shrugged and said, "You confirmed her suspicions."

"Grandma never asked you about it after that?"

"I guess it was easier to pretend it never happened."

Maybe for them, I thought. No more pretending for me.

"Grandma stayed for you. And your mom," he said fiddling with his keys, "was not herself."

He leaned against the wall and sighed loudly. "She blamed me for Hal's death."

"So she was pissed," I said. "So what? It doesn't mean you should abandon your injured wife for someone else. You took advantage of both of them. You make me sick!" And just like that, a wave of nausea came over me and I ran to the sink and threw up.

Dad was right there, trying to rub my back, but I shook him off. Instead of returning to the table, I stayed at the sink and kept my distance.

He went back to leaning against the wall, rattling his keys out of habit. "Look, Kennie, there's a lot you don't know about that time, and it's not my place to tell you everything, but I can tell you my part."

I came alive. "Don't you dare blame any of this on Mom! She's been hurt enough."

He looked at the keys in his hand, rearranging them as he talked. "Okay," he said. "Here's my part."

I waited for it.

"After helping Gail get back on her feet—"

"Just say it! You had an affair. She got pregnant. You kept it a secret!"

His head jerked up like I'd slapped him.

"Just facts, Dad."

He paced back and forth along the kitchen island between us, drumming his fingers rhythmically. "Here are the facts, and I only speak for myself." He stopped in front of me, and I stepped back until I was against the counter.

"Your mom was injured. That's a fact. And she was distant . . ."

"What are you talking about?" I asked.

"She stopped speaking to me."

I rolled my eyes.

"You were having a lot of emotional problems after the accident, and so was your mom. She was depressed."

I opened my mouth, but before I could speak, he said, "That's a fact."

"When did you start the affair with Gail?" I asked.

"A couple of months after," he said. "She got pregnant right away."

I shivered, trying to get the thought out of my mind. "Did Mom find out?

He nodded.

I took a step closer. "She knows?" I grabbed the edge of the island for support as it hit me hard: I was just finding out what everyone else already knew.

"Did Uncle Steve and Aunt Mimi know, too? Am I the only one who never knew?"

"I was going to tell you so many times. I tried, but I couldn't do it, Kennie." He poured himself another drink and downed it. "I didn't want to lose you." He covered his face and sobbed.

Everything was a lie.

This was not my dad. He didn't cry. I stayed where I was, unmoved by his emotion.

As fast as it started it stopped, and as he recovered I could hear his barely audible counting. That got me, and my eyes welled up again. I wanted to bolt, but Mom walked in. I ran to her and hugged her hard. "I'm so sorry, Mom. I'm so, so sorry."

She murmured something and put her keys on the table.

"Kennie," she said, looking at the floor.

"It'll be okay, Mom," I said. "It's over." I quickly reconfigured the family: Mom and me in a condo, and Dad in Portland. With them.

She looked at Dad. He shifted on his feet, hands in his pockets. I felt a change in the air.

"What? A divorce? No kidding. You don't have to break it to me gently," I said.

"There's more, Kennie," Mom said.

I held my stomach and looked from Mom to Dad and back at Mom. She took a deep breath and blew it out.

"Don't try to make it better, Mom," I said.

She shook her head and sat down at the kitchen table.

Covering her face, she said, "It's not as simple as Dad was bad, Mom was good." Now she was the one crying.

I brought a tissue box over and sat across from her. "It's going to be okay, Mom, I know it will." I waved a tissue in front of her, and she wiped her eyes and blew her nose.

"Kendra, listen to me," she said. There was an edge to her voice.

"Mom," I whispered, bracing myself.

"We were best friends. Gail, me, your dad, and Hal. The four of us did everything together," she said, bursting into tears again. "In the beginning, it was just Gail and me. Then she married Hal, and Dad and Hal became close—best friends, too."

Dad sat down at the head of the table. I didn't acknowledge him but instead took Mom's hands and squeezed them. "I'm so sorry, Mom," I said, imagining the devastation she felt—the betrayal.

"At first it was great. We sailed every weekend. We cooked meals and went places together. You probably remember," she said, smiling weakly.

"I remember, Mom," I said.

"I don't know exactly when things changed, but it was sometime after you were born. Gail and Hal had tried everything to have a baby, and they couldn't. It drove a wedge between them."

I thought of Jilly.

"The more they fought, the more Hal came over to see us. For support."

Dad cleared his throat.

"Even when Dad wasn't home," she said.

I looked at him. He was fiddling with his keys again.

"Hal and I became close," she said, twisting her tissue.

It was a few seconds before I got it, but when I did, I was up and at the door.

"I'm so sorry, Kendra," Mom said. "Hal and I fell in love. Nobody knew."

I looked at Dad. I couldn't read him.

"When he drowned, I blamed your father."

She was crying again, but I couldn't feel anything for them. A wall was coming down, and I wanted it to.

I stayed at the door, ready to leave if my questions weren't answered.

Mom got up and came toward me.

I put my hand up. "Stop." I needed to think, and her hugging and crying was confusing me. Dad's phone vibrated. He turned it off and looked at me.

"I don't get this," I said, indicating them together, as a couple.

"It probably seems crazy, but we're married, and even though it's unconventional, we love each other, Kendra," Dad said.

"Just not in the traditional way," Mom said.

Her upbeat tone set me off. "What?" I said, going to the counter for support. "Please don't." I shook my head. "Just tell me straight?"

Dad stood and motioned to Mom.

Mom nodded and sniffed.

"We could've gotten divorced, but we loved you and we loved our family," Dad said. "We stayed together in full knowledge of what we had done and what we were doing."

Mom cleared her throat. "Kendra, we stayed married to the *family*. Our family."

"But what about his other family?" I wasn't buying it. "He was living a lie, even if a couple of people knew the truth!"

That shut them both up. We sat in silence for a few minutes.

"I know," Dad said. "The older you and Jilly got, the easier it was to lie about it."

"We were going to tell you so many times," Mom said.

I went back to the door.

"Please wait," Mom said. She rushed to me and hugged me even while I stood stiff and motionless. "Just know that we both love you and we'll do whatever we need to do to make it right again."

I opened the door. It would never be right. It never was right. It was a lie.

I WAS AT THE COSTELLOS', IN JENN'S BED, WHEN the door cracked open in the middle of the night.

"I'm back," she said, elbowing her way under the covers. We hugged and she said, "Tell me everything."

I caught her up. Even about Will. She was oddly silent. It wasn't the Jenn response I'd expected.

"I guess I did have a Breakout Summer, just not the kind I'd planned," I said.

I heard her sigh into the dark. "Me too. Doug broke up with me."

"What?" I took her hand.

"No, let me correct myself. Doug's mom broke up with me."

I made a sound, somewhere between a laugh and a choke.

"She said that he was feeling smothered by me. According to her, my energy sucks his energy, and when I'm around, he can't find his creative life force."

We held each other and laughed until Bo pounded on the wall.

"But the funny thing is," she said, "that's kind of true. I was totally energized when I was with him. But I never felt it going the other way—like he was feeding off my energy."

I gasped. "Me too. With Will, I mean."

When it was quiet, I said, "But not with Bo. I'm myself
with Bo."

———————————

THE NEXT MORNING I WOKE EARLY. THE COSTELLOS'
kitchen smelled of fresh coffee, and I could see that Mrs. C.
had left for work already. I grabbed a mug and sat on the
front stoop.

I had an odd feeling as I looked over at my house, like it
belonged to someone else. When I was young and I was over
here and I'd hear my parents on the screened porch having
drinks and laughing, I'd think how it was sad that the Costellos weren't part of their group. I'd feel sorry for Jenn and
Bo's parents. Especially after their divorce.

I'm ashamed to admit it now, but I felt better than them.

Behind me I could hear Jenn making breakfast noises.
"I'm bringing out a refill and an epic coffee cake," she said.

"Good idea," I said. I swallowed my last sip and set the
mug on the stoop.

The door opened, and as soon as she sat down, I started
in with the panicky feelings. "I don't want to deal with it. I
just want to stay here and pretend they don't exist."

"You were going to stop doing that, remember?" she said.

I gave her a look. "I've got every reason to panic," I said.

"And you have every reason not to." She broke off a couple

of pieces of coffee cake and gave me one. "You know how to deal with your anxiety now, and you'll be moving out and going to college. But how's Jilly going to deal with all this?"

I wondered. What about Jilly? Before I could answer, Bo texted me from the kitchen.

> **Bo:** I miss you.
>
> **Me:** I miss you, too xo
>
> **Bo:** Can we go somewhere and be alone? I heard what happened and I want to make sure you're okay.

Jenn leaned back and hollered through the screen door, "If that's my brother, tell him he can have you to himself in ten minutes." She hovered close while I texted and pretend-groaned like she was disgusted with us, but I could tell she thought it was sweet.

> **Me:** I'll be okay as soon as I'm with you ☺
>
> **Bo:** Living room in ten?
>
> **Me:** Living room. I've got cake.

Jenn stood up and sighed. "You guys are over the top. Cute, but over the top."

CHAPTER 22

YOU THINK A LIE IS A SINGLE THING THAT YOU DO, but it's alive, and before you know it, that lie is in charge. When I took that first snapshot of my dad and Gail, it changed everything. It changed me.

Two months ago, I was the girl who used to divide life into *before the boat accident* and *after the boat accident*. Now I'm a quasi-Buddist. Staying in the moment keeps me from looking at things *before* or *after* the affair. It's hard not to fall back into the habit of sorting events into categories and catastrophes.

A counselor helped me learn that a feeling is just a feeling and I don't have to react to everything. How it works is I try to let things pass through me instead of letting things stay inside me and turn to anxiety. I've been doing a lot of feeling exercises lately. Saying things like "Hey, Anger and Resentment, I see how you're here, and now you can move on."

It sounds silly, but it's helping.

It's not that being mad about what Mom and Dad did is a bad thing. I should be pissed, but it shouldn't turn me into Angry Girl, like it's my superpower. And now that I get that, I know I was wrong about one thing.

I told them—yelled at them—that our family had never been right, that it had been a lie. Now, two months later, it's come to me how many things *were* right about my family.

Like love. As bad as the secret was, there was always love in the family. Sometimes it felt strict, like making me stay home when I was overtired, or hard, like when Dad and I would work through an anxiety attack. But usually it was laughing together at the dinner table or sitting quietly and sharing the paper on Sunday.

And now there's Bo. When I'm with him I have no secrets to keep, there are no lies holding me hostage, and we tell each other everything without censoring it.

Since that big talk in the kitchen, when I learned the truth, I've been slowly moving toward forgiveness. When I'll actually get there, I don't know, but I think Jilly will have something to do with it.

At first she and I were pretty formal around each other.

We had a meeting with all of us together at the table, like one of those parent-teacher meetings where everyone is on their best behavior. Jilly was so fidgety that I thought someone was going to say something, but the adults didn't notice; they were focusing on each other.

When I saw her staring at my camera, I whispered, "Do you want to see some pictures?" They were her soccer pictures. The only ones I'd saved.

She jumped up and we went onto the screened porch and looked at the photos of her making goals and dribbling down the field.

Now we see each other a few times a week. I've shown her how to use my camera, and she's teaching me how to play soccer and the violin. I can do no wrong in her eyes.

I'm her cool big sister.

And being her older sister makes me want to be better than cool. I want to be stronger.

I'm getting there, and Bo is making it easy and fun. He's helping me replace my frightening boat memories with happy ones. It started when we took his boat out in the cove, at first staying close to shore in case I was scared, but each time we went out it got easier, and soon I was driving. The last time we went out, we made it around Beach Rose Island to the open ocean, the late-day sunlight putting our island in silhouette. I couldn't remember seeing the back side of the island before, and now I'd captained the boat there! I was still realizing what I'd just done when Bo took the wheel and handed me my camera. I'd forgotten to take a picture.

He was right. It was a snapshot moment.

Click.

ACKNOWLEDGMENTS

Thanks go to:

My editor, Christy Ottaviano at Henry Holt, whose keen eye and insightful remarks were the right combination of questions, comments, and adorable stickers. Thank you for helping me shape Kendra's story.

My agent, Wendy Schmalz, who found this story the perfect home. I am forever grateful for your guidance.

My PW's, who saw the many incarnations of *A Lie for a Lie*. Your friendship and encouragement are invaluable. Argh, mateys!